Grey Cloud

Grey Cloud

Charlotte Towner Graeber

illustrated by Lloyd Bloom

FOUR WINDS PRESS   NEW YORK

WITHDRAWN

Library
SW. OK. St. U.
Weatherford, Oklahoma

To my mother, Phyllis Young

With special thanks to Sam Ciacco of the
Elgin Homing Pigeon Association

LIBRARY OF CONGRESS CATALOGING IN PUBLICATION DATA

Graeber, Charlotte Towner.
  Grey Cloud.

  SUMMARY: Tom resents his family's move to the
country until he meets a strange, quiet boy who
raises racing pigeons.
  [1. Pigeons—Fiction. 2. Friendship—Fiction]
I. Bloom, Lloyd. II. Title.
PZ7.G75153Gr   [Fic]   79-14673
ISBN 0-590-07600-0

Published by Four Winds Press
A division of Scholastic Magazines, Inc., New York, N.Y.
Text copyright © 1979 by Charlotte Towner Graeber
Illustrations copyright © 1979 by Scholastic Magazines, Inc.
All rights reserved
Printed in the United States of America
Library of Congress Catalog Card Number: 79-14673
1 2 3 4 5 83 82 81 80 79

jF
G 734g

1

The shrill of a police whistle jolted Tom from his sleep. In the city the sound meant something was happening in the neighborhood—something exciting and maybe dangerous.

"That's the boy, Diamond. Good boy!" Carrie's voice came loud and clear across the farmyard.

Tom stuffed a pillow over his head. It was only his sister, Carrie. She wore the whistle around her neck and blew it whenever she wanted her horse to obey a command.

The pillow didn't help, and Tom gave up. He pulled on his clothes and headed downstairs to the kitchen. Mom stood at the stove.

"Pancakes and good country sausage," she said, setting a plate on the table.

Tom slid into his seat. One good thing about living in the country was Mom's having time to cook breakfast again.

"When you finish, you can go into town with Dad," she said.

"Into Coatsville? Aw, Mom, have a heart," Tom said. He had seen enough of Coatsville in one trip to last a lifetime.

"You don't have to go," Mom said, swiping at the table

229027

with her dishrag. "But you could make an effort to be a part of things around here."

Mom was upset. Tom finished the sausage on his plate and stood, trying to think of something to say.

"Thought I'd work on the pasture fence this morning," he offered. "Some places are pretty bad."

Mom straightened the kitchen chairs. "Well, that's a start anyway. If you give it a chance, this place might even grow on you."

Tom shrugged and stepped outside. Except for Carrie's whistle and Dad's banging around in the machine shed, it was quiet—so quiet you could probably hear the corn growing, like they said.

"No way," he muttered. "No way this place will ever grow on me."

He jammed his fists into his pockets and started across the farmyard. Inside the machine shed Dad was leaning over an old tractor with a grease gun.

Tom had to admit the country agreed with Dad. He looked strong and not a bit tired.

"Going into town with me this morning?" his father asked.

"Thought I'd start on the fence," Tom said, looking around the shed.

"There's a roll of fence wire on the shelf," Dad said, "and the cutters are on the workbench."

Tom found both and started out of the shed. Now he had to work on the fence for sure. Still, anything was better than wandering around Coatsville while Dad priced fertilizer and looked for parts for the tractor.

The wide gate to the pasture stood open and, beyond, the fencing seemed to stretch endlessly. At one time the place had been a boarding stable for horses. With some repairs Dad hoped to use it for that again.

Tom walked to the first break in the fencing. It took almost an hour to wire the fence together. When he stood up, the sun was high. He wondered what Joe and Sammy were doing. Playing handball against the back of Barney's pool hall? Riding the elevated train across town to watch the Sox play an early game? Tom picked up a small stone and hurled it toward a distant fence post. It fell about a yard short. He picked up another and took aim at a post a few yards closer.

Just then a movement in the grass near the bottom of the post caught his eye. He had seen a few gophers and field mice since they moved here; maybe he had stirred one up with his first throw. He lowered his arm and watched. Soon the tall grass moved again, and Tom started toward it. As he came nearer, the activity on the ground increased.

Finally Tom stood looking down in the grass at a bird. It flapped its wings helplessly and fixed its round eyes on Tom in a frightened stare. It was a pigeon. Tom certainly knew a pigeon when he saw one. Pigeons had roosted on the back porch of their old apartment in the city. Pigeons populated the ball parks and the museums and the school grounds. What was one doing here in the middle of a pasture?

Tom reached down to touch the pigeon. "Are you hurt?" The pigeon stared back at him.

Gently he lifted the injured bird in his hands and oddly it did not struggle to get away. Instead it lay quietly, watching him. Tom saw now that the pigeon was different from the city pigeons. It was smaller and more handsomely marked. Light-grey wing feathers faded into pure white at the tips, and the neck was banded in dark

grey. The tail feathers seemed to shine almost silver in the bright sunlight.

And it *was* hurt. The pigeon held one leg stiff, and dried blood crusted the white leg feathers.

"Poor fella. Got to get you fixed up," Tom said.

He started back across the pasture holding the injured pigeon close to his chest. At the pasture gate Carrie spotted him and ran across the yard, leading Diamond on a rope.

"What have you got, Tom?" she called.

"Keep your horse back," Tom warned.

Carrie tied Diamond to the fence and came over.

"Why, it's a pigeon—a plain old pigeon," she said.

Tom kept walking toward the house. "It's a pigeon all right, but not a plain one. I know it."

In the house Mom placed a newspaper and an old towel on the table, and Tom put the pigeon down. First it flopped on its side. Then it righted itself and sat blinking at them and turning its head from side to side.

"I think its leg is broken," Tom said. "Maybe it was shot or something."

"Maybe it ran into something when it was flying," Carrie said.

For once Tom was glad Dad had been raised on a farm and knew about animals. He said, "I think we should wait until Dad gets home. He'll know what to do."

Mom soaked a small piece of bread under the faucet and held it near the pigeon's beak. First the pigeon ignored the soggy bread, but soon it began to eat.

"No telling how long the poor thing was lying there," Mom said.

When Dad came home, they were all watching the pigeon eat. It would grab the bread with its beak, then cock its head to swallow.

"What have we got here?" Dad asked. Without another word he picked the pigeon up and looked him over. "Looks like the leg was hit with a BB gun," he said. "It's broken."

With a wooden matchstick and a clean piece of torn rag Dad made a tiny splint for the pigeon's leg.

"Say, did any of you notice this other leg?" he said. "It's got a band on it clear as day."

Tom leaned close to see what Dad was talking about. Sure enough, a small metal band encircled the pigeon's good leg.

"What does it mean?" Tom asked.

Dad put the pigeon back down on the table. "It means the pigeon belongs to someone," he said. "Someone who values it and wants it back."

Tom shrugged his shoulders but he felt an odd pull at his chest. Somehow he had figured on keeping the pigeon, without really thinking it outright. Now the pigeon probably belonged to someone else.

"Orville Breen raises pigeons," Carrie said.

Tom tried to think who Orville Breen was. Then he recalled the tall, thin boy who got on the school bus at the end of Huntley Road each morning. His hair stuck out like broom bristles, and he wore glasses thicker than window glass.

"Better call Orville and see if he's missing a bird," Dad said, heading for the shed.

Tom looked hopefully at Mom.

"Well, it can't sit on my table all day," Mom said. "I'll call while you fix a temporary place for it in the barn."

The pigeon cooed and lay resting against Tom's arm as he carried it back outside.

In the barn Tom lined a cardboard box with old papers and lowered the pigeon into it. "I hope you don't belong to anyone, Pretty Boy," he said.

Back in the house Mom set a bowl of steaming gravy on the table along with chicken and mashed potatoes. "I can't imagine anyone being without a phone," she said. "But there is no one named Breen listed in this area."

"Lots of people have unlisted numbers these day," Dad said. "It keeps the salesmen from pestering them."

Tom piled fried chicken and potatoes on his plate. He was glad that Orville Breen was not in the phone book. At least he could keep the pigeon a while longer.

"I'll ride my bike over to Huntley Road in the morning," he said. "That's where Orville Breen gets on the bus each morning. He has to live somewhere nearby."

That evening Tom took fresh water and a handful of cracked corn out to the pigeon. The bird was settled deep in one corner of the box with its head tucked under a wing. When Tom reached in with the seed, the pigeon popped his head out and began squawking.

"It's all right, Pretty Boy," Tom said softly. "You are safe here."

The pigeon peered at Tom, then stretched for a piece of the corn Tom held in his hand.

Tom watched as the pigeon pecked at the rest of the corn. Then he let his fingertips rest on the pigeon's soft grey head. "I'd name you Pretty Boy if you were mine," he said. He wondered what Orville Breen called the pigeon if it was really his.

2

Early the next morning Tom hurried to the barn to check on the pigeon. When he stepped to the box, the pigeon popped his head up, eager for the corn Tom held out to him.

"You're doing fine," Tom said. He checked the tiny splint on the pigeon's leg and smoothed the feathers along the pigeon's neck. He wished he could just keep the bird for himself and forget about the leg band. But he had promised to find out if the pigeon belonged to Orville Breen. He wheeled his bike out of the garage and pedaled to the main road. The morning air was cool and fresh, and somewhere in the distance a church bell chimed.

When Tom reached the stop where Orville Breen got on the school bus each day, he stopped. There was only one road leading away from the main highway. That was Huntley Road, all gravel, and rough from wear. Tom pedaled down the road, looking at the mailboxes as he passed. The first box belonged to someone named Hecht, and the farm beyond was large and neat. The next mailbox said THE MASONS, and a long drive led to a farm almost hidden by bushes and trees. Tom pedaled on to where the gravel road turned abruptly to the south. At the turn stood an old farmhouse, a sagging barn, and several other small buildings. The mailbox was old, and Tom could barely make out the first letter of the name on the side. It was a B and had to stand for Breen. Tom rode into the farmyard and leaned his bike against a tree near the house.

Just then he heard sounds coming from the direction of an old chicken coop. It was the sound of birds—pigeons like Pretty Boy. Tom crossed the yard listening. When he reached the coop, he looked through the open door and saw Orville Breen standing with a pure-white pigeon on his forearm. Another grey-and-white pigeon perched on his shoulder.

"Coo, boys," Orville Breen said. His voice was almost a whisper.

Tom stood looking in at the makeshift coop with its dirt floor and slanted roof. Pigeons were everywhere. They perched near the unpainted ceiling and along both sides of the coop. When Tom stepped inside, they all scattered, squawking loudly.

Orville Breen turned to stare at him. His eyes blinked behind his heavy glasses, and his face seemed angry.

"I'm sorry I frightened your pigeons," Tom began. "I just rode over on my bike a few minutes ago."

For a moment Orville continued blinking. Then a frown filled his long and bony face.

"Pigeons don't like strangers," he said.

Already the white bird had resettled on Orville's arm. The rest of the pigeons continued to cluck and coo. Tom stood near the door feeling out of place and awkward.

"What's the white pigeon's name?" he asked, not knowing what to say.

Orville stroked the pigeon's snowy wings with his hand. "This here's Snow Arrow," he said.

Tom stepped forward to admire the pigeon. "I'm Tom Herrick. Over on Bode Road," he said.

Orville nodded but said nothing. Tom guessed everyone knew who he was by now. Dad said news travels fast in the country. People didn't have much else to talk about except who came and went. Tom wondered if Orville was going to say anything more. Maybe he didn't like to talk.

Tom noticed that one whole wall of the coop was lined with rows of wooden boxes. Each square box had the front open and held its own feed container. He watched as Orville stepped to the boxes and filled each cup with a mixed feed. Then Orville lifted a bucket of water to fill several watering trays attached to the opposite side of the coop.

"What I came for—" Tom began. "I found a pigeon on our place yesterday morning."

Orville continued to fill the water trays.

"It's got a broken leg, and a band on the other one. I thought it might belong to you."

Orville picked up a broom. "I lost one a few days ago," he said. He began sweeping the floor near Tom's feet.

Tom shuffled backward out of the way. Wasn't Orville interested in his pigeon? Didn't he want to know if the bird was all right? Orville finished sweeping and placed the broom on a hook behind the door.

Tom scuffed his feet on the dirt floor. "The pigeon? You want him back?"

Orville turned to stare at Tom. "Might be my bird. Might not," he said. "I'll come over to your place as soon as I finish my chores."

For a while Tom stood watching Orville with his pigeons. But the tall, thin boy acted as though Tom was not there. Tom felt uncomfortable and he stepped to the door of the coop.

"See you later then," he said.

Orville Breen wiped his hands on his torn overalls, nodded, and turned away.

Tom stepped outside into the sunlight wishing he had never said a word. He jumped on his bicycle and wheeled out of the farmyard, angry and alone. As he passed the scattered farm buildings and new-plowed fields, he hardly saw them. He longed to be with Sammy and Joe back in the city—riding around the old neighborhood looking for empty pop bottles and old beer cans.

He passed a farmer driving a tractor down the middle of the road and he started to wave. But the farmer pulled his hat over his eyes and looked straight ahead. Tom lowered his hand. He hated the country and all the country people. They were stubborn and unfriendly, and Orville Breen was the worst of all.

At home he parked his bicycle and hurried across the yard. Inside the darkened barn the pigeon scratched at the side of his box, and Tom reached in to touch him. He stroked the smooth head as the pigeon's golden eyes blinked at him.

"Joe and Sammy should get a look at you," he said. He could almost hear Sammy saying something funny about pigeon droppings.

A slow ache filled Tom's chest as he thought of his friends in the city and the fun they always used to have together. He wanted to grab the pigeon and hold him tight against his chest. Instead, he cupped his hands around the warm feathered body and lifted the pigeon out of the box. Then he sat for a long time holding the pigeon in his hands and talking to him softly. He wished Dad had never had the heart attack that forced him to move his insurance office to the country. He wished they had never found this place Mom called Peaceful Acres.

Just then Tom heard his father's voice from the back porch. "Anyone want to go fishing?" he called. "There's a river just five miles south of Coatsville."

Tom sat quiet and still with the pigeon in his arms. Dad would drop a fishing line in the water and sit for hours watching the bobber and dozing in the sun. Tom heard the truck start up and pull out of the yard. He did not want to sit on a riverbank all day being peaceful. Besides, he had to stay and wait for Orville Breen.

Tom waited all afternoon. Finally, at four o'clock, he saw Orville Breen coming down the road on an ancient bicycle with old balloon tires. When he turned into the drive, Tom saw that he carried a small cage in the bicycle basket.

"I've come to look at the pigeon," Orville called. He leaned the bike against the porch where Tom waited.

For a moment Tom stood unmoving on the porch steps watching a spider swing from the railing. He could be as unfriendly as the next guy.

Then Orville Breen stepped forward. "I have to hurry back. Milking time," he said simply.

Tom nodded and started toward the barn, with Orville loping behind him. Inside, Tom pointed to the cardboard box. "The pigeon's over there."

Orville crossed the barn, and the pigeon started cooing and hopping around excitedly. It was Orville Breen's pigeon, all right.

"That's a good boy," Orville almost whispered as he

lifted the pigeon out of the box. The pigeon cooed softly as Orville stroked its wings. Orville held out the broken leg.

"That's a right good splint," he said.

"My dad put it on. He knows all about things like that."

Orville nodded and held the pigeon close. "We best be getting on home, Grey Cloud," he said.

Grey Cloud! Tom had to admit that was a better name than Pretty Boy. And it fit the pigeon, too. He was as grey and soft-looking as an April cloud. Tom waited for Orville to thank him for returning the bird. But Orville Breen stood looking out of his thick glasses for a moment, then walked outside to his bicycle. He placed the pigeon, Grey Cloud, in the small cage.

Tom watched from the barn door as Orville tied the cage in the basket with an old rope. He wished he had never looked for the pigeon's true owner.

Orville straddled the old bike and headed out of the yard with Grey Cloud. Suddenly Tom had a frightening thought. What did Orville Breen do with the pigeons he kept in the old coop? Was he raising them for meat?

"Wait!" Tom called as Orville reached the main road.

Orville Breen looked back from the mailbox.

"What do you do with the pigeons?" Tom yelled.

Orville shaded his eyes from the sun as he looked back at Tom. "I race them!" he answered.

Tom watched as the old bicycle disappeared from sight. Had he heard right? Did Orville Breen race the pigeons he kept at the old farm over on Huntley Road?

3

Tom waited at the end of the driveway with Carrie on Monday morning. He hated taking the school bus. In the city it was just a few blocks to school—a quick walk with Joe and Sammy. Out here it took almost an hour on the stuffy bus to get to Kane Consolidated School.

Carrie scrambled onto the bus giggling and calling to her friends. Tom sat down in the front. The boys in the middle of the bus were in his own classes. They all held jackets and books on their laps and were laughing and joking among themselves.

Tom wished the family had moved in the summer instead of during the school year. He didn't know anyone. He was left out of everything. He glanced toward Carrie and envied the way she got to know everyone so quickly.

As the bus neared Huntley Road, Tom saw Orville Breen waiting near the highway. Tom had not noticed the tall, gangly boy much before, but now he watched as Orville stepped onto the bus. When Orville started past him, Tom caught his arm.

"Hi, Orville. How is Grey Cloud?"

Orville turned, startled. Then he made his way to the back of the bus without saying a word. There he folded his long legs into a corner seat and rested his large hands on his knees. For the rest of the ride, Orville Breen sat looking out of the dirty back window.

What was with him anyway, Tom wondered. Hadn't he tried to be friendly? And he wanted to ask more about the pigeons and how Orville raced them. But now he wished he had never spoken to the strange boy. Orville Breen did not want to be friends and that was that.

At last the bus turned into the huge parking lot behind the school, and everyone piled out. Tom let the others shove around him until the bus was almost empty. Carrie laughed as she pushed past with her friends.

When Tom finally stepped off, he found himself face to face with Orville. Orville's thin face was flushed, and his eyes looked like large green marbles behind his thick glasses.

Tom started to turn away but Orville held his arm. "You can come see Grey Cloud," Orville said.

Tom stood with his mouth open, then nodded. Before he could say anything, Orville turned and hurried across the parking lot with his arms swinging at his sides.

The rest of the day Tom looked for the tall figure between classes. He wanted to tell Orville he would come after school and see Grey Cloud. But the school was large, and Tom did not see anyone he knew except Carrie. She promised to tell Mom and Dad that he would be late getting home from school. Tom had already made up his mind to get off the school bus with Orville that afternoon.

After school Tom climbed on the bus and found Orville already sitting in the back.

"I hope it's okay," Tom said. He wedged into a space next to Orville. "I thought I'd visit Grey Cloud on my way home."

Orville shrugged and turned to look out of the window as usual. At Huntley Road Orville headed for the door, and Tom grabbed his jacket and followed him off the bus.

"Hey, wait up!" Tom called, as Orville walked down the gravel road ahead of him.

Orville turned. "Hurry up, then," he said. "I got chores." Then he moved quickly on down the road.

Tom halfway wished he hadn't gotten off the bus at all. Maybe he should have waited until another day to see Grey Cloud. Now he had to run to keep up with Orville's long strides.

At the farm Tom followed Orville across the yard and to the house. Without a word Orville went inside, leaving Tom at the back door.

"Orville? That you?" a woman's voice called. A short, plump woman in a pair of men's overalls stepped out of the barn. She seemed surprised to see Tom standing on the porch.

"I'm Tom Herrick," Tom called. "My folks bought the Reamer place."

The woman stood, uncertain, then pushed a strand of wiry hair away from her forehead. A large black-and-white cat sauntered out of the barn behind her, and she reached down to scratch his ear. Just then Orville banged out of the house, dressed in the same torn overalls he'd worn the day before. He scooped up the cat and put him in the kitchen.

"The bolt on the barn door needs fixing," the woman called to Orville.

Orville nodded. "I'll take a look, Ma, soon's I see to my birds." He stuffed a biscuit in his mouth and handed one to Tom. "Come on," he said. Tom followed Orville across the yard to the old chicken coop.

Inside, the pigeons greeted Orville eagerly, cooing and stretching their wings wide.

"Coo, boys. Coo, girls," Orville said softly.

The pure-white bird called Snow Arrow settled on Orville's arm and rubbed his beak against Orville's sleeve. Tom looked around the coop for Grey Cloud among the other pigeons.

"Where is Grey Cloud?" he asked finally.

Orville stepped to one cage at the end of the bottom row and lifted the grey pigeon out. Grey Cloud cooed and bobbed his head up and down. Gently Orville checked the tiny splint on his leg.

"Can I hold him?" Tom asked.

Orville shrugged and handed the pigeon to Tom. As Tom took Grey Cloud in his hands, the pigeon blinked his yellow eyes and cocked his head sideways.

While Tom held Grey Cloud, Orville stepped to the far end of the coop and unhooked a rectangular door above his head. He lifted the door and latched it open to the ceiling. Sunlight and fresh air streamed through. Immediately several pigeons flew through the opening to the outside.

"Won't they get away?" Tom asked.

"Won't go far from the loft," Orville muttered. "Haven't had their supper yet."

Orville had called the old coop a loft. Tom thought that had a nicer sound than coop. He looked out the door and saw the pigeons flying above and around the loft.

"Got to get their exercise," Orville said.

Tom nodded. Last night he'd asked Dad about racing

pigeons. Dad told him it was a sport and that pigeon owners raced their fastest birds for prizes. It involved a lot of training and work. Tom was about to ask Orville how he trained his birds when Orville said, "Got to get the chores done."

Orville took Grey Cloud from Tom and placed him in a screened area in the sunlight. Then he stepped outside and closed the loft door.

Tom offered to help with the chores. But Orville just hurried across the yard, serious and quiet as usual.

For almost an hour Tom followed Orville around the farm. He watched the pigeons soar overhead while Orville fixed the broken latch on the barn door. Was Grey Cloud all right inside the loft? Tom stood near the fence while Orville fed the pigs and turned on the water to fill their watering trough.

Mrs. Breen worked in the barn milking two cows while Orville swung fresh straw into their stalls. The short, round woman and gangly Orville made a strange pair. Tom wondered where Orville's father was, or if there was a Mr. Breen at all. From the looks of the farm, there had been no man around the place for some time.

Tom leaned against a horse stall. Suddenly Orville handed him a pitchfork. "Want to feed the horses?" he asked. Tom glanced at a pair of reddish-brown horses swishing their tails and stamping behind their stalls. "I guess so," he said. Orville pointed to a bale of hay lying nearby. Tom gripped the pitchfork, leaned forward, and plunged the fork into the middle of the bale. When he pulled it out again, the hay scattered in all directions. He had never handled a pitchfork before. It was awkward. He tried again. This time the fork stuck in the bale.

Orville began laughing, holding his sides and slapping his overalls.

"Sure ain't no farmer," he said.

Tom felt his cheeks burn as he pulled the pitchfork out of the bale of hay. Then Orville grabbed the end of the handle and showed him how to bend and swing the hay over into the stall. Tom managed to do it right after that.

"It's easy once you get the hang of it," Orville said.

After the horses were fed, Orville filled a bucket with oats and poured clean water for the horses. Tom wondered if they would get back to the pigeons at all. Finally Orville hung the bucket on a peg and started out of the barn. He ducked into the loft and came back out with a coffee can. Tom watched as Orville began shaking the can over his head and calling to the pigeons. One by one the loose birds flew back toward the opening in the loft roof. Orville hurried inside and the pigeons dropped through the opening one by one. Orville opened the can and began filling the feed cups in the pigeons' cages. When they were all back inside the loft, he reached up and lowered the door over the opening again, hooking it securely. Tom saw that the pigeons could not get out through the roof when the traplike door was latched in place.

Nothing could get into the loft through the opening either. Tom thought of the huge cat that roamed the farmyard. The latch was a good idea.

When they stepped out of the loft again the sun was low over the fields and pastures.

"I'd better be getting home," Tom said. He planned on calling for a ride home. "Can I use the phone to call my dad?" he asked.

Orville shook his head. "Got no phone."

Tom remembered Orville Breen was not listed in the telephone book. For a moment he stood looking toward the road as Orville leaned against a fence post. It was going to be a long walk home, and his stomach grumbled. He shrugged and started off. "See you later then," he called to Orville.

He was halfway up the drive when Orville pointed to the ancient bike leaning against the porch and shouted, "Take it!"

Tom hurried back to the porch, jumped onto the wobbly bike seat, and pedaled to the road. At the mailbox he turned to wave back at Orville. But the farmyard was empty; Orville had already disappeared.

Tom got up earlier than usual the next morning. He wanted to return the old bike to Orville Breen before school. And he hoped to spend a few minutes in the pigeon loft with Grey Cloud and the others. He wheeled the bike out of the yard and started down the road. The April air was brisk, and a smell of fresh-plowed earth hung in the coolness. Tom breathed deeply and zipped his jacket against the chill. On a fence post a red-winged blackbird sang out, and overhead a hawk circled the field looking for something to eat.

When Tom reached Orville's farm he leaned the bike against the porch where he had found it. For a moment he stood looking around. The place was really neglected. Paint peeled from the house and the barn, and the back porch was sagging. Tom heard voices in the kitchen, then Orville banged out of the back door.

"I brought your bike back," Tom called cheerfully.

Orville yawned and pushed his glasses high on his thin nose.

"I thought you might need it today."

Orville nodded, picked up a bucket, and stepped to the pump. He lifted the handle up, then pushed it down hard. Fresh water gurgled from the spout into the bucket. Tom stood watching. Didn't Orville ever have anything to say? Didn't he feel like talking sometimes? Back in the city Joe and Sammy were always going on about something.

"Okay if I look at the pigeons?" he asked.

Orville yawned again. "Guess so. Long as you're here."

Tom hurried to the loft and stepped inside. "Coo, boys. Coo, girls," he said, trying to sound like Orville.

Snow Arrow peered at Tom from his cage in the middle row, and Grey Cloud poked his head out at the far end. The other pigeons moved about nervously. Tom stood in front of Snow Arrow and held out his arm, hoping the white pigeon would come to him. But Snow Arrow sat where he was, blinking his round eyes. A dozen other pigeons cooed and walked about their cages uncertainly.

Tom stepped to the cage where Grey Cloud sat with his broken leg held stiff in the tiny splint. Slowly Tom reached forward with his hand, and the grey pigeon sat watching. Tom smoothed Grey Cloud's dark head and touched his wing with his fingertips.

"That's my boy," he said softly.

All at once Grey Cloud rubbed his head against Tom's outstretched hand. The feathers felt soft and warm.

"Good boy," Tom said.

Then Orville was at the door, saying, "School bus will be coming!"

Tom patted Grey Cloud's head once more and hurried out of the loft. Orville closed the loft door, then started off across the yard. Tom had to run to keep up with him.

"Grey Cloud came right to my hand!" Tom hollered.

"Pretty soon he'll be hopping on my arm just like Snow Arrow."

"Pretty soon you'll be missing the bus!" Orville yelled back. Orville was running now, his long legs spanning almost four feet with every step. Tom saw the space between them grow wider.

"Hey, wait up!" he yelled.

In the distance the school bus came into view as it rounded a curve. Orville reached the main road just as the bus pulled to a stop at Huntley Road. Tom tried to run faster. He was going to miss the bus for sure. He watched the door swing open and Orville climb on. Then Orville stood holding the door until Tom reached the road and climbed on behind him.

Without a word Orville turned and walked straight to the back of the bus. For a moment Tom stood at the front trying to catch his breath. Then he started down the aisle. As he passed the boys in the middle, one of them looked up at him and made a crazy face—just like Sammy used to do all the time. Tom grinned and walked back to join Orville.

It was funny. Tom had been at Orville's farm twice, but Orville was still like a stranger. On the bus he sat stony and silent, with his face pressed close to the dirty window. Orville Breen was a mystery all right. But one thing was sure—he knew about pigeons.

The rest of the week Tom was kept busy at home helping his father with the fence work. As soon as everything was ready, his dad planned to buy two more horses.

Each morning Tom waited at the front of the school bus until Orville got on. Then he followed him to the back of the bus and sat down. Tom couldn't understand why

Orville chose to sit at the back all the time. The exhaust fumes made him sick, but there was no explaining the ways of Orville Breen.

On Friday morning Orville turned to Tom as he sat down. "Took Grey Cloud's splint off," he said.

Tom squeezed on the seat beside Orville. "Is he flying? Do you let him out with the others?"

Orville nodded. "Good as new," he said.

That afternoon Tom got off the school bus with Orville. "I'll feed the horses for you," Tom said as he hurried to keep up. He didn't want Orville to think he was going to hang around doing nothing.

When they reached the farm, Orville headed for the house again. This time he stopped on the back steps and turned to Tom. "Want to come on in?"

Tom followed Orville into a cluttered and sunny kitchen. Dishes filled the sink by the window. Books and magazines covered a large round table. And in the corner the huge black-and-white cat dozed on top of the clothes in a laundry basket.

Orville dropped a schoolbook on top of the others and opened a breadbox on the counter. "Have a biscuit?" he said, handing Tom two and stuffing one in his own mouth. Then he went upstairs to change his clothes. For a moment Tom stood alone in the room watching the cat and munching on a biscuit.

"That you, Orville?" Orville's mother came into the kitchen holding a greasy wrench in one hand and an old rag in the other. She was wearing overalls, and a man's blue handkerchief was tied around her greying hair.

"It's me again," Tom said.

Mrs. Breen wiped the rag over the wrench in her

hand. She seemed embarrassed and uncertain.

"Orville's changing his clothes," Tom said.

"Pump broke again," she said. Just then Orville came back with his mouth full of biscuit.

Orville reached out for the wrench without speaking. It was easy to see where he got his silent ways all right. Tom guessed that if there was any talking to be done, he would have to do it. He took another bite of biscuit, ate it quickly, and said, "Good biscuits, Mrs. Breen. Best I've ever had."

Unexpectedly Orville leaned forward and patted his mother's arm. "Ma makes good biscuits, sure enough," he said. Then he walked across the kitchen and out of the back door with Tom behind him.

In the loft Orville opened the trap to let the pigeons fly free. "This here's called open loft," Orville said. "Open loft gives the birds freedom to come and go for a spell each day." It seemed Orville was more eager to talk when it was about pigeons.

"Can't I do something to help?" Tom asked, as they headed for the barn. "You'd get done with chores faster that way."

Orville eyed him doubtfully. But inside the barn he handed Tom a wide shovel from a peg on the wall.

"You can start on the stalls," he said. "Need cleaning."

Tom peered into an empty stall where half a dozen dairy cows were kept. Now they were out in the pasture grazing in the April sun. The hay on the floor was matted and soiled, and Tom held his nose. "Pheweee," he said. "What do I do?"

Orville nodded to a wheelbarrow just outside. Then he pointed to a pair of boots by the door. "You wear the boots, shovel into the wheelbarrow, and haul it out back." Orville went off to fix the pump, leaving Tom in the middle of the stall.

Tom wished he hadn't offered at all. Cleaning out a cow stall was going to be a smelly and dirty job. He tried to think of other things as he scooped the first shovelful of manure and dirty hay into the wheelbarrow. Beneath the mess, huge earthworms lay wiggling and slimy. Tom gulped and scooped again.

By the time Orville got back, Tom had cleaned two stalls.

"That's enough for one day," Orville said. He climbed a ladder up into the top of the barn and threw down a fresh bale of hay. He came down and cut the wire around the hay. Swinging a pitchfork easily, he pitched hay over the top of the stalls. Tom watched as Orville filled each stall with fresh hay and spread it around over the clean floor.

"Guess I'm no farmer, like you said," Tom said. He felt foolish and awkward next to the strong tall boy. All at once Orville began to laugh. He laughed so hard he had to sit down on the bottom rung of the ladder. The sound was deep and bubbling and full. It was almost worth cleaning out the smelly stalls just to hear Orville laugh that way.

Tom began laughing, too. Still, he was glad the smelly job was done for today. Orville got up and started across the yard.

Tom watched this time as Orville filled the coffee can with pigeon feed. It was a mixture of dried corn, peas, and a little rice. Orville stepped outside shaking the can rhythmically over his head. When the pigeons heard the sound, they headed toward the loft. It was something to

watch them circling. Each pigeon glided lower and lower until it dropped onto the outside perch and popped through the trap. Inside, Orville filled their feed cups from the large can in the corner.

Tom scooped a handful of seed on his own hand as Grey Cloud hopped through the trap. He held his arm out to Grey Cloud. For a moment Grey Cloud sat just inside the trap, bobbing his head to and fro. Then he hopped onto Tom's forearm and began eating the seed.

"Orville!" Tom called. "Grey Cloud came right to me."

Orville turned from the cages. Snow Arrow sat on one shoulder, and another white pigeon with dark-grey shadings perched on his head. "He's extra hungry, I'd say."

But Tom shook his head. "No. He likes me. He really likes me. And I bet he is a good racing pigeon, too."

Orville turned back to the cages with Snow Arrow still on his arm. "Done all right last year," he said.

Tom waited, wanting to know more. But Orville finished putting out feed, closed the trap, and began sweeping the floor.

Finally Tom's curiosity got the best of him. "When do you race the pigeons?" he asked. "And how?"

Orville stopped sweeping. "I'll be taking them out in the morning," he said. His green eyes squinted behind his glasses, and he pushed his pale hair off his forehead. "Come over early if you want."

5

Tom could scarcely get through breakfast Saturday morning. He gulped a bowl of cold cereal and grabbed his jacket. His bicycle seemed to eat up the road as he headed west over the open countryside.

Orville was already in the pigeon loft when Tom got there. "About to leave without you," he said.

Tom nodded. It was only six-thirty, and the sun had hardly warmed the ground yet. Near the door of the loft sat a large wire cage. Quickly Orville cupped Snow Arrow in his hands and placed him inside.

On the perch at the front of his box, Grey Cloud hopped around excitedly. "You fed them already?" Tom asked.

"Don't get nothing till they get back," Orville said. He cupped his hands around a white bird splashed with grey across its head. "Good girl, White Rain," he said.

Tom liked the way Orville had all of his birds named. Their names fit the way they looked, and sounded gentle, too. Blue Boy was a male of a blue-black color. A female with a white head and grey wings was called Light Feather.

Orville placed a solid-grey pigeon named Sun Shadow in with the others. Tom wondered how many pigeons he would put in the cage—and if Grey Cloud would be one of them now that his splint was off. Orville reached for one more pigeon sitting deep in his box. "Come, Silver Bow," he coaxed. The pigeon bobbed his white-and-grey head as Orville put him in the cage.

"What about the others?" Tom asked. "What about Grey Cloud? Isn't he ready to fly yet?"

Orville shrugged. "Can't race them all this year." He glanced at Grey Cloud. "Go on. Put him in with the others."

Tom lifted Grey Cloud off his perch and carried him to the cage. Altogether there were six pigeons in the cage when Orville slid the wire door shut and fastened it. Then he carried the cage outside.

"Where are we going?" Tom asked, closing the door behind him.

Without a word Orville crossed the yard to an old garage and opened the sagging doors to reveal a rusted black truck. Tom heard the truck start up and watched it back out of the garage. Orville pulled the truck around smoothly so that he was facing out of the driveway before he brought the truck to a stop.

Then he got out and slid the cage of pigeons into the back of the truck and covered it with a canvas tarp.

"Hey! Where are we going anyway?" Tom asked again.

Orville swung his long frame back into the driver's seat. "You comin' or not?" he called out to Tom.

Tom scrambled into the other side, wondering if Orville could possibly be old enough to drive.

Orville pushed his left foot down on the clutch and eased the gearshift forward. Soon they were bumping and rattling out of the farmyard and onto Huntley Road. Orville steered the truck around the curve and away from the main highway.

Tom had gotten used to the strange quietness of Orville Breen. But still he wondered where they were going. And he wanted to know how Orville had learned to drive.

They had gone about five miles or so when Tom asked, "How far are we going anyway?"

Orville looked straight ahead. "A ways yet," he answered. It seemed they drove endlessly—past scattered farm buildings, dark fields, and open pasture land.

After passing several miles of woodland, Orville slowed down. He turned onto a dirt road which was almost hidden by brush and dry weeds. They rattled along until they came to a clearing, and Orville stopped the truck.

"Where are we?" Tom asked as he looked around. To the north a woods stretched to a set of farm buildings in the distance. And to the south an old gravel quarry dropped off into craggy rocks and wild bushes below. Orville was in the back of the truck lifting the tarp off the pigeons. "What happens now?" Tom asked, climbing up onto the back beside Orville. Orville opened the cage door. "It's time to let the birds go."

Tom understood. Orville was going to let the birds free to fly back to the loft on their own. He watched as Orville reached into the cage for the first pigeon. It was White Rain. He cupped her in both of his large hands, lifted her above his head, and tossed her into the air. Tom watched the bird fly higher and higher over the old gravel pit. Then she turned and headed straight east across the clearing. In a few minutes she disappeared beyond the trees. Next, Orville lifted Snow Arrow out and released him with a gentle toss upward. The pure-white bird flew in the same pattern as White Rain, his wings wide and shining in the early sunlight. Tom watched until he was out of sight.

"Why don't you let them go all at once?" Tom asked.

"Some folks do it that way," Orville said. "Some use single toss." Single toss, Tom thought. That meant letting the pigeons go one at a time. Tom was learning more and more about racing pigeons, even though he had to get it from Orville one bit at a time. Grey Cloud was the last pigeon to be released. Tom admired his sleek wings lifting against the blue sky.

Orville jumped off the back of the truck and climbed into the front again. "Hurry up!" he called. Tom stood watching until Grey Cloud could be seen no longer.

"Got to get back before the first bird comes in!" Orville shouted.

Tom hurried into the truck. Soon they were on the Huntley Road again. "How far did we come?" Tom asked.

Orville looked ahead. " 'Bout thirty miles. Maybe more."

The rest of the way Orville sat concentrating on the road. When another car approached from the opposite direction, Orville sucked in his breath. It was just a farmer heading out to his fields. Tom wondered if Orville had a license to drive yet. But he said nothing.

Orville drove faster going back, and soon they were close to home. Tom held onto the dashboard in front of him as Orville swerved around the last sharp corner. The truck bounced into the farmyard and Orville pulled next to the loft and jumped out. Tom sat catching his breath as Orville stood looking to the south.

Then Tom saw why Orville had been in such a hurry. Over the trees a small dot grew larger and larger. Was one of the pigeons coming back already? Tom jumped out of the truck and stood beside Orville, watching. He hoped the bird would be Grey Cloud, but surely that wasn't possible. He had been let go at the very last.

Orville ran into the loft. He opened the trap and came out with the blue coffee can in his hand. He began shaking the can above his head as hard as he could. Tom was sure the pigeon could not hear the sound while it was so far away. But still Orville shook the can. Then he began calling. He made a soft whistling sound through his teeth and called, "Coo, coo."

Tom wished he had Dad's binoculars so he could see which pigeon was coming. Soon another bird appeared over the same trees. Tom felt his blood racing as the first bird got close enough to see. It wasn't White Rain, the first pigeon to be set loose. But it wasn't Grey Cloud either. It had to be the other grey pigeon, Sun Shadow. As the bird neared the loft, it stretched its wings wide and glided downward.

Orville shook the can, whistled some more, and stepped inside the loft. Tom waited, watching Sun Shadow drop to the outside perch. The bird sat listening. Tom could hear Orville inside shaking the can. Sun Shadow heard too, cocked his head, and popped through the trap.

Tom saw three or four pigeons in the sky, coming home. The next one to drop to the roof was Snow Arrow. Without hesitating, he went directly into the loft. Tom squinted and shaded his eyes against the bright sky.

"Grey Cloud," he called. The next pigeon was Grey Cloud! He circled briefly, glided downward, and settled on the perch. Tom raced inside, calling and trying to whistle the way Orville did. At once Grey Cloud popped through and headed for the seed Orville had placed in his box.

"He came in third!" Tom said. "He left last and he got back third!"

Orville nodded, holding Snow Arrow on his arm. Then he shook the pigeon off and went back outside.

At last all six pigeons were home and safely in the loft. The last one to come home was White Rain. Tom asked Orville why she took longer than the rest.

"Might have stopped off somewhere," he said.

Tom held Grey Cloud on his arm, stroking his wing feathers gently. Grey Cloud hadn't stopped off anywhere. "Is Grey Cloud your best racer?" Tom asked.

Orville stood quietly, with a faraway look in his green eyes. "Reckon it's Snow Arrow here," he said. "Both birds got good breeding. Championship stock."

Tom wanted to ask more, but Orville turned suddenly away. He took off his glasses and wiped at them with a corner of his old checked shirt. Tom felt uncomfortable, so he put Grey Cloud in his box and began sweeping the floor. What was wrong with Orville Breen anyway? Did he just have a piece of dust in his eye?

"What next?" Tom asked, stepping to the door of the loft.

Orville put his glasses on, then he stepped outside and climbed back in the truck. Tom watched Orville drive into the garage. Orville closed the garage doors and turned to Tom. "Going out again tomorrow," he said.

"Okay. I'll be here by six this time." Tom walked to his bicycle and headed out of the yard. It was against the law to drive before you were fifteen. Orville Breen was really looking for trouble.

6

The next morning Tom woke up to the alarm clock he had set the night before. For a moment he lay listening to the crows as they called high over the oaks. Next the wakening sounds of a dozen different birds filled the air. Tom was getting used to the sounds of the country. He dressed quickly. In the kitchen he grabbed Dad's binoculars and a handful of cookies. Then he hurried outside to his bicycle.

His legs felt strong as he wheeled out of the yard toward Orville Breen's. He liked the rich smell of young fields and the way the sun threw its first light across the pastures. All around, trees and roadside bushes held their new leaf buds up to the sun. Somehow he did not feel lonely as he pumped along the roads this morning.

When he arrived at the Breens', Orville was standing on the porch feeding the black-and-white cat a biscuit.

"Hey! I'm early!" Tom shouted.

Orville finished, and they crossed to the loft together. Inside, the pigeons blinked their round eyes and murmured softly.

Tom stepped to Grey Cloud's perch. "Wake up," he said.

Orville opened the wire cage on the floor and placed White Rain inside first. Next he lifted Snow Arrow from his perch.

Tom cupped Grey Cloud in his hands. "You'll beat them all today," he said. Grey Cloud brushed his head against Tom's arm while Orville placed the rest of the pigeons in the cage. Finally Tom put Grey Cloud in with the others.

Orville backed the truck out of the garage and pulled it around. Tom slid the cage of pigeons on the back and covered it. Soon they were rattling down Huntley Road in the direction of the old gravel pit. Orville kept his eyes on the road as they bumped along. Tom decided to find out more about racing the pigeons.

"When do you race?" he asked.

Orville scratched his head. "Start the end of May. Go till fall," he said.

Tom nodded. "Well, how far do they race, anyway?"

Orville blinked behind his glasses. "Depends. Hundred, two hundred miles."

Tom looked out at the countryside. Two hundred miles! That seemed a long way for pigeons to fly. What if they didn't all get back in one day? He thought of Grey Cloud lying injured in the pasture. Some dog might have found him first.

At last they reached the turnoff to the gravel pit. When they stopped, Tom jumped out of the truck before Orville had even turned off the ignition.

"Let White Rain go first," Orville called.

Tom uncovered the cage and reached inside. He guessed Orville wanted to give White Rain a head start. Gently he cupped the small grey-and-white bird in his hand. Her eyes seemed more red than golden as she blinked up at him. He touched his fingers to the top of her grey-splashed head.

"Good girl. Hurry home," he whispered. Then he lifted

her high and tossed her into the air. He watched until
she disappeared beyond the trees. He hoped she would
not stop anywhere along the way this morning.

Orville climbed onto the back of the truck and reached
inside the cage for Grey Cloud. Tom watched as Orville
held him high and released him.

"Good boy. You'll show them," Tom called as Grey
Cloud flew higher and higher. The pigeon banked grace-
fully, turned into the sun, and then headed toward home.

Orville released Snow Arrow next, and then Sun
Shadow. Soon all six pigeons had disappeared beyond
the trees. Tom climbed back into the truck as Orville
started the engine. As the truck rattled along the road
Tom felt himself dozing. But Orville took the last turn
like a race driver, and Tom bolted upright. They were
both eager to get out of the truck. Orville ran to open the
trap and get the can of seed.

Tom took the binoculars from his pocket and adjusted
them. Except for a few blackbirds, the sky looked
empty. Then Tom saw them—two dots growing larger
and larger. He hoped one was Grey Cloud.

Orville came out of the loft, shaking the can. Tom
squinted through the glasses. The pigeon in the lead was
white, but was it White Rain or Snow Arrow? At first it
was hard to tell. Soon Tom could see the pure-white
wings of Snow Arrow rising and falling in a steady
rhythm. Grey Cloud was right behind him.

"Come on, Grey Cloud. Come on!" he shouted.

The two pigeons flew almost side by side. They circled
the loft together and glided downward. Orville dashed
inside, shaking the can and whistling.

Tom watched both pigeons drop onto the outside perch

at the same time. He raced inside. "Come on, Grey Cloud. Come on."

Snow Arrow popped through the open trap. Grey Cloud hopped through next. Tom was disappointed. Grey Cloud had been released ahead of Snow Arrow. But somewhere along the way Snow Arrow had overtaken him.

"He beat you; Snow Arrow beat you, Grey Cloud."

"Don't matter," Orville said unexpectedly.

The grey pigeon pecked at his feed and blinked his yellow eyes.

Tom knew Orville wanted all of his birds to fly well. But he still wished Grey Cloud had come in first. He wanted him to be the best.

Soon the rest of the pigeons were back in the loft drinking eagerly from the water trays. All except one.

"White Rain is missing," Tom said.

Orville nodded. Then he stepped outside to search the sky once more. Tom looked through the binoculars, squinting hard. Maybe White Rain was lost. Maybe she was lying injured in a field somewhere, like Grey Cloud.

"Shouldn't we look for her?" Tom asked at last.

"She'll be coming along," Orville said. Then he turned away and started for the barn.

"But aren't we going back to find her now?" Tom called.

Orville shrugged his shoulders. "Got chores to do," he said simply.

Tom felt angry and helpless as he watched Orville cross the yard. White Rain could be anywhere. Surely they should look for her. "Guess I'll go then," Tom said.

Orville watched from the doorway of the barn as Tom

jumped on his bicycle and pumped to the road. But instead of turning toward home, he headed back along Huntley Road. He would look for White Rain alone. For over an hour Tom tramped through one field and another. He parked his bike at the side of the road and scanned every clump of brush and weeds with the binoculars. But there was no sign of the small white pigeon anywhere. It was hopeless. If she was lying in a field, he could walk right by and never see her. At last he got on his bicycle and headed for home.

For the rest of the morning he helped Dad clean the old stalls in the barn for the new horses. Then he sat on the porch staring toward the pasture where he had first found Grey Cloud. He wished Orville had a phone like everyone else. Then he could call and see if White Rain had returned.

Finally after lunch he headed back to Orville's. When he got to the farm he went right to the loft. Grey Cloud and the others greeted him. But White Rain had not come home—her perch was empty.

Tom marched to the house and knocked firmly. At once Orville's mother came to the door; she held the huge cat in her arms. "Orville's out," she said quietly.

Tom glanced about the farmyard but heard no sounds from the barn or the garage. "Where is he?"

Mrs. Breen pointed beyond the farm buildings. Tom turned and ran in the direction she had pointed. He climbed the fence at the end of the pasture and shielded his eyes. Then he pulled out the binoculars and looked again. But Orville was nowhere in sight. For a while Tom crossed the fields and pastures going directly west. He understood that Orville was looking for White Rain, following the direct flight line west. Tom walked through a wooded area; when he came out into the sunlight, he was looking across another field. He lifted the binoculars and searched the area until he saw Orville, walking steadily and fast. Tom hurried, hoping to catch up, but Orville was too far ahead. For a while Tom followed behind, looking through the binoculars in all directions—he might find some sign of White Rain that Orville had missed.

After a while his legs began to ache and he sat down to rest. When he got up again, he saw that Orville had stopped, too. He peered through the binoculars and saw Orville kneeling beside a ditch near the road.

"Hey, Orville!" Tom called. But Orville was too far ahead and did not look up from the ditch. Tom felt a small knot of fear form in his throat. Had Orville found something there by the road? He began running and his heart pounded hard. Soon he was close enough to see Orville's face as he leaned toward the ground. It was dark and solemn.

"What is it?" Tom called.

Orville did not answer, and Tom hurried closer. Now he saw that Orville held something in his large rough hands. It was White Rain! Dry blood caked the white wing feathers, staining them a terrible red. Her eyes were closed, and her head fell sideways in death.

Tom heard his own cry shatter the quiet morning. Sobs rose in his throat, and he could not hold them back. Then he heard a low moan and looked at Orville's face. It was twisted and pale with anguish. Tears spilled over the bony nose and down the thin cheeks. Tom reached out to touch Orville's shoulder and felt it tremble.

"She's dead!" Orville cried once. His voice was sharp

and bitter. He held a finger to a gaping wound in the pigeon's side, and Tom looked away. He felt sickened and helpless.

For a long while they knelt together beside the ditch; then at last Orville stood up and started back across the field. Tom followed. Orville held his shoulders rigid and his back straight as he marched along holding the dead pigeon inside his jacket. At the farm he climbed over the last fence and headed for the old garage. He stepped inside and closed the door behind him.

For a moment Tom stood staring at the garage; then he went inside the pigeon loft. He glanced at White Rain's empty perch and could not get the picture of her lifeless body out of his mind. Tears filled his eyes.

Silently he filled the feed cups and water trays as the other pigeons cooed around him. At last he cupped Grey Cloud in his hands and held him close. It might have been Grey Cloud instead of White Rain. For a long while Tom stood smoothing the pigeon's feathers.

It was late afternoon when Tom climbed on his bicycle and headed home again. As far as he knew, Orville was still sitting in the old garage with the dead pigeon in his arms.

Who would harm a gentle pigeon, he wondered? Why would anyone want to shoot a shy and beautiful thing? But as he pedaled along, he remembered the city pigeons. People were always throwing rocks and junk at them because they were so messy. Once he and Joe had watched Sammy hit a pigeon with a rock and knock it to the ground. "Bull's-eye!" he could almost hear Sammy shouting.

They never found the pigeon Sammy hit; they had never even looked to see if it was dead or alive.

7

Monday morning Tom climbed onto the school bus right behind Carrie. He was anxious to see Orville and tell him he was sorry about White Rain. He started down the aisle of the bus to wait at the back for Orville. As he reached the middle, someone grabbed his sleeve.

"Hey! Why don't you sit here for a change?" It was Gary Stevens.

"Come on," Gary said. He squeezed over, making room for Tom.

Tom was surprised; he slid into the space. What would it hurt to sit with Gary until Orville got on the bus?

"Hey, what do you want to sit with creepy Orville every day for?" Gary asked.

"Yeah," a boy named Shorty said. "It stinks back there, too."

Tom shrugged his shoulders. He wanted to tell them he sat there because no one else was friendly. And that he liked Orville. But he said nothing. As the bus neared Huntley Road, Tom squirmed in his seat. He watched Orville climb on the bus and start toward the back.

Tom lifted halfway out of the seat, but Gary yanked him back. "Come on, Tom. Orville Breen is a creep."

Tom glanced up just as Orville passed them. Orville

couldn't help but hear what Gary had just said. Still, his face was closed. Without hesitating, he continued to the back and sat down.

For a few minutes Tom sat with Gary and the others. As they talked about sports and their favorite baseball teams, Tom's head began to ache. He couldn't forget the remark Gary had made right in front of Orville. Orville was strange, all right. Tom knew that as well as anyone. But he was not a creep. Finally Tom swung his legs into the aisle of the bus.

"Hey! Where you going?" Gary asked, grabbing Tom's arm.

Tom stood up, pushed Gary's hand away, and headed for the back of the bus. He squeezed beside Orville. "They wanted me to sit with them awhile," he said, trying to sound easy.

Orville nodded and looked out the window. "I buried White Rain at the edge of the woods," he said.

Tom studied his shoelaces and frowned. "Do you think someone shot her on purpose?" he asked. "Grey Cloud, too?"

Orville shook his head. "Hard telling." He turned back to the window.

Gary and the others sat turned in their seats, watching them from the middle of the bus. When Tom looked up, Shorty made a face like a crazy person. Tom just looked away. When the school bus reached the parking lot, the boys waited until Tom and Orville got off.

"Hey, Tom," Gary called, "come on and walk with us."

Shorty and a boy named Dave crowded close to him, acting friendly. "Your locker is right near mine," Shorty said.

Tom watched as Orville walked on without him. Then he started across the pavement with the others.

"What do you do after school?" Dave asked. "Do you like to hang around in the gym?"

Tom shrugged. "I guess."

"We hang around shooting baskets and wrestling," Shorty said.

Tom began to feel better. He liked sports. In the city he had been good at wrestling and swimming. He just hoped Gary and Shorty wouldn't make any more cracks about Orville.

At the lockers everyone separated and went on to their classes.

"See you after school, then," Gary called.

Tom nodded. It would be fun to fool around with a bunch of guys again. He thought about Joe and Sammy back in the city. Shorty even looked a little like his friend Sammy. Acted like him, too—always joking and making faces.

Tom didn't see Orville all day. He had planned on going to Orville's to help with Grey Cloud and the other birds after school. But he could go tomorrow instead. Besides, he needed more than one friend at Kane Consolidated.

After school Gary, Dave, and Shorty met Tom at his locker and took him down to the gym.

Gary headed straight for the trampoline and began jumping and twisting in the air. Dave and Shorty wrestled on a floor mat while Tom watched.

"Hey, you guys. Look at this!" Tom turned in time to see Gary do a double flip on the trampoline.

"Are you on the gymnastics team?" Tom asked. He wished he could do as well as Gary.

"Naw," Gary said. "You have to practice every day. The coach makes you do push-ups and run around the track about fifty times."

Tom wondered what was wrong with that. He would like to be on a team and working out every day.

Gary sat on the edge of the trampoline, tying one sneaker. "I got better things to do."

"What do you do?" Tom asked.

Dave and Shorty stopped wrestling.

"Hang around. Just hang around." Gary said.

Tom began to feel right at home. It was almost like being with Joe and Sammy again.

All at once Gary got off the trampoline and rolled onto the wrestling mat with Dave and Shorty. "Come on. I'll wrestle you," Gary said to Tom. Dave and Shorty scooted off the mat.

For a minute Tom stood looking down at Gary. Then he flung himself at Gary on the mat. But Gary was strong. Tom felt his left leg buckle as Gary grabbed it and threw him to the mat.

"Yeah. That's our boy!" Shorty laughed.

Tom felt his face burn as Gary twisted his ankle hard. Next Gary grabbed at his head and hooked one arm around his neck. Tom felt small and foolish lying beneath Gary's sweaty hands. At last Gary let him go and stood smiling down at him.

"You should be on the wrestling team," Tom said, rubbing his leg and neck where Gary had held him fast.

Gary laughed. "Like I said I don't like team sports. Besides, this summer I'm gonna get me a motorbike."

"You're not old enough," Tom said.

Dave and Shorty laughed out loud and banged their hands against the trampoline.

"You don't need a license to ride on your own place," Gary bragged. "I ride my brother's all the time." Tom had to admit that having a motorbike was something special. He wanted to tell Gary and the others that Orville Breen could drive a real truck. But he kept quiet. They all thought Orville was a creep.

At five o'clock the janitor came to lock the gym. Gary and Dave walked out together, and Shorty walked with Tom.

When they passed the main office, Tom stopped to use the phone. "Got to call for a ride," he told Shorty.

Shorty and Gary laughed. "Just hitch, like we do," Gary suggested.

But Tom had already dialed, and Dad answered. "Maybe next time," Tom joked.

He watched the three boys walk to the main road and stand waiting for a ride. When Dad pulled in with the blue truck, he ran across to meet him.

"Something special at school tonight?" Dad asked.

"Just messing around with some guys," Tom said. Dad turned and patted his shoulder roughly. "I knew you'd make more friends soon," he said.

Across the school grounds Gary and the others climbed into a station wagon that stopped for them. Tom knew what Dad would say about hitching rides from school.

Tom knew what Dad would say about Gary calling Orville a creep, too. Well, it felt good being with a gang again. He'd missed Joe and Sammy. And besides, kids were always making cracks about guys like Orville. It was the way things were.

That night Tom lay awake thinking of the fun he'd had after school. He didn't like the way Gary had pinned him to the wrestling mat right off and twisted his ankle deliberately. But he guessed Gary was just showing off, the way guys did with new kids, when he talked about getting a motorbike, too.

Tom thought about how Orville took the turns in that old rusty truck of his. Maybe, if he asked, Orville would teach him how to drive. Maybe he would know how to drive before Gary even got his old motorbike. That would be something, all right.

8

The next day Gary, Shorty, and Dave were waiting at Tom's locker after school.

"Want to wrestle again?" Gary challenged.

Tom wanted to get even with Gary for twisting his ankle, so he followed them to the gym. He could stop at Orville's later in the week.

In the gym Tom hurried to the mat and stood waiting. "Ready?" he called as Gary stepped to the mat.

Gary gave a wild yell and flung himself at Tom's legs. But this time Tom was ready for him. He swung forward, grabbed Gary around the middle, and turned him onto his back on the mat. For a minute Tom knelt over Gary, leaning on him with all his weight. Gary tugged and struggled, but Tom had him.

Suddenly Gary began yowling. "My leg, my leg!" He groaned and moaned as though he were in pain.

"What's the matter with your leg?" Tom asked, still holding him flat against the mat.

"Got a cramp. Let me up," he moaned.

Tom released Gary slowly and stepped back.

Jumping up, Gary said, "I could have gotten out of your hold. Cramp got me bad, that's all."

Tom decided he did not like Gary very much. Gary

knew full well that he was down. He used the excuse of a cramp because he couldn't stand to lose. Shorty slapped Tom on the shoulder, laughing. "You can't win with old Gary here," he said. "Ask Dave!"

Dave watched silently as Gary hopped around the gym, rubbing his leg and swearing.

"Hey, Tom," Gary called. "You still hanging around with that creep, Orville?"

Tom nodded. "We get along."

"The guy's got a screw loose," Shorty said. "Fooling around with a bunch of silly birds." He started making noises like a chicken.

Tom shrugged. "Orville Breen is okay," he said. He wondered what they knew about Orville's pigeons.

"Okay?" Gary shrieked. "Okay, my foot. He's just like his old man. Crazy as a coot."

Tom stepped forward holding his hands in fists against his thighs. "What do you mean by that crack?" he demanded.

Shorty said, "You're new here. Everybody knows old Breen is locked up in a nut house somewhere."

Tom stood clenching and unclenching his fists. He never thought about Orville's father—except to know that he wasn't around. He guessed Mr. Breen was dead or had gone off somewhere a long time ago. It didn't seem important.

"The nut house?" Tom looked from Shorty to Dave.

"Yeah." Gary was swaggering across the gym. "The bug house, the loony bin—take your pick."

Dave told him, "Orville Breen's father has been in the state hospital for over a year."

Tom felt sick and frightened. He wanted to run out of the gym and straight home. But he stood stiff and silent, looking at the boys around him. Could it be true?

"He flipped out one day while he was mowing hay," Shorty said.

"He fell right on the ground, twisting and flinging around like some sick animal," Dave added.

Tom could only stand and listen. Maybe Orville's father *was* sick somewhere. But that didn't make him crazy. "Maybe he's just sick!" he argued.

"Sick in the head, all right!" Gary said. "And creepy Orville is just like him. Crazy as they come."

Tom knew Orville was not crazy. If anyone was nuts, it was Gary, faking leg cramps, bragging about buying a motorbike.

"Orville Breen is not crazy!" he yelled. "He is smart enough to race pigeons and he can drive a truck already!"

Immediately Tom wished he had never spoken. Three pairs of eyes stared back at him.

"He ain't old enough!" Shorty said.

"Yeah," Gary said. "You're making it up."

Tom glared at Gary, who seemed ugly and stupid. "Orville knows how to drive a stick shift, and so do I!"

With that he turned and walked out of the gym to wait for Dad at the back of the school. He felt like a fool, telling them about Orville's driving. He hoped he had not started any trouble for Orville—or for himself.

On the way home he asked Dad about the state hospital.

"Orville's father is there," he said. He explained what Shorty and Dave had said about Mr. Breen.

"It could be a number of things," Dad said. "Why don't you just ask Orville?"

But Dad didn't know Orville Breen. You couldn't ask him right out something like that.

When he got on the school bus the next morning, Tom hoped Gary and the others would keep quiet and leave him alone. Shorty made a face like an idiot, and Dave nodded silently. Gary just looked straight ahead without speaking, and Tom went on to the back of the bus.

Near Huntley Road, Tom looked out to see Orville. He was wearing a red cap. Tom held his breath as the bus stopped and Orville climbed on. He hoped Gary would keep still for a change and say nothing to Orville as he passed. Orville didn't seem to hurry as he walked to the back of the bus, but his glasses slid down on his thin nose.

"Hurrah, it's Friday," Tom said, trying to be cheerful. "Okay if I stop by after school?"

Orville nodded. If he cared about Tom's staying after school with the others, he said nothing. Instead, he turned his face toward the dirty window.

As the bus rolled toward school Tom watched Orville. What was it like having a father away for over a year? Tom knew how he felt when Dad was rushed to emergency for his heart attack last summer. But a whole year without your dad? And how did Orville feel when people made cracks and called his father crazy? Tom tapped Orville on the shoulder.

"Can't wait to see Grey Cloud again," he said.

After school Tom hurried to his locker before the others could get there. Then he went directly to the parking lot to wait for Orville and the bus.

At the farm Tom followed Orville to the loft. When they stepped inside, Grey Cloud cooed and murmured low. Tom stepped to the perch and held out his arm for the grey pigeon.

"I think he missed me," he said. Grey Cloud hopped onto his arm, bobbing his head from one side to the other.

Orville reached up and unlatched the hook that held the trap shut. Most of the pigeons hopped right through, anxious to enjoy the late April sunshine. Tom carried Grey Cloud out and tossed him into the air. His light-grey wings shone almost silver as he glided and banked above the farmyard.

Just then Orville stepped out of the loft blinking and scratching his head. "Got to go for some dried peas," he said, walking to the old garage. As he opened the garage door, the black-and-white cat scooted around the corner. Orville scooped him up and carried him to the house. "Ma, keep old Caesar inside while I'm gone." Orville's mother stepped onto the porch and took the huge cat into her arms.

Orville got the truck, and Tom jumped in beside him.

"Where do you get the feed?" Tom asked.

"Fella over your way. Races a few birds, too," Orville said.

Tom watched Orville shift into first gear from neutral. He pushed his left foot onto the clutch pedal, then gave the truck gas with his right. The old truck eased onto the road as smooth as glass.

Tom wished he could drive. When they came to a crossroad stop, he worked his own feet along with Orville's. First press the clutch all the way down. Shift into gear. Then let up the clutch and ease down on the gas pedal. It seemed easy enough.

Orville shifted into gear and turned onto another road.

"Sure wish I could drive," Tom said. He watched Orville steer the old truck around another turn.

"Driving ain't hard," Orville said, watching the road ahead. But he did not offer to let Tom take the wheel of the truck.

Finally Orville turned off the road onto a rutted back lane. The truck bumped and rattled until they came to a farm not visible from the main road. Rough wood fences stretched as far as Tom could see, and in the middle sat a house among the towering oaks. H. H. WITTER, was printed on the mailbox at the main drive. Orville drove into the yard.

A man dressed in an old tan jacket and bright-green baseball cap stood raking the area around a huge loft. It was almost as big as the house, with an outside deck on the side.

Orville got out and walked over. "Come on," he called back to Tom.

"Afternoon, Orville," the man said, looking up. "Ain't seen you since last fall."

Orville nodded. "Came for some of your dried peas."

As Tom stood waiting, a dozen or more pigeons glided and circled over the loft. And on the roof a dozen more sat sunning and dozing in the late-afternoon sunshine.

The man leaned the rake against the loft and walked to a storage shed nearby. "How're your birds coming along, Orville?" he asked.

Orville followed the man, and Tom waited near the loft. He had never seen so many pigeons. Several looked just like Snow Arrow, and one bird could have been Grey Cloud's twin.

When Orville and the man came out of the shed, Orville carried a large gunnysack. The man smiled at Tom and spat tobacco juice on the ground.

"Who's your friend here?" he asked. Orville stood silent and stoney, and Tom felt awkward. The man stepped forward and held out a freckled hand. "Mr. Witter, son. Fellow pigeon racer and friend."

Tom held out his own hand. "Tom Herrick," he said. "My folks bought the Reamer place this spring."

The man nodded. Then he turned to Orville. "Say, I'm taking a bunch of my racers out tomorrow. You like to bring some of your birds along?"

For a moment Orville's face darkened. Then he gave a brief smile and nodded.

"I'll be leaving for Savannah around six. I'll stop for you on my way."

Orville fished in his overalls and handed Mr. Witter a crumpled bill. "I'll be ready," he said. Orville climbed in the truck and started the engine.

Tom got in slowly. He had hoped to get a look inside Mr. Witter's loft. And he wanted to know more about his pigeons, too. But Orville didn't seem to like Mr. Witter much. He turned the truck around in the driveway and headed back to the main road.

"Where's Savannah?" Tom asked, when they reached the road. "Why are you taking the pigeons there?"

Orville stopped, looked both ways, and turned the truck homeward. He pushed his thick glasses up on his nose and scratched his ear.

"Savannah's two hundred miles south. A lot of races start from there." He slowed the truck down as they got close to a tractor. Then he stepped on the gas and passed it easily.

Tom admired the way Orville handled the old truck.

He wondered how he had learned to drive so well. And he wondered again how Orville got away with driving when he wasn't old enough.

At the loft Tom filled the water trays with fresh water while Orville mixed the peas with corn and rice to make new feed. When it was time to leave for home, Tom glanced at the truck parked in the yard. He wanted to ask Orville about his driving. He wanted to ask if he could go along to Savannah the next day. Instead, he walked to his bicycle.

"Think you can get here by six?" Orville called from the doorway of the loft.

"You bet!" Tom shouted back.

9

At five-thirty in the morning the sun eased over the horizon. Tom stretched, yawned, and stumbled to the kitchen through the darkened house. He smelled coffee. In the kitchen Dad sat at the table oiling his fishing reel.

"I'll drive you over," Dad said. "I'm fishing at White River this morning."

Tom was glad for the ride early in the morning. On the way he watched Dad's face light up as he pointed out a mare and her colt in the refenced pasture and talked about another horse he planned to buy. Dad was happy, and stronger, since they had moved from the polluted city air.

At Orville's, Tom jumped out at the mailbox and hurried across the yard. Orville was already in the loft. The wire cage was open, and Snow Arrow and Blue Boy were already inside. Tom stepped to Grey Cloud's perch and held out his arm. Grey Cloud looked around and then pecked the bottom of his empty feed cup.

Tom laughed. "Nothing to eat till you get back." Even the water trays were empty, and Tom wondered why. He was about to ask when Mr. Witter's truck turned into the yard. "Be right there," Orville called. He placed Sun Shadow and Silver Bow into the cage. Tom cupped Grey Cloud in his hands and placed him with the others.

Outside, Orville's mother stood near the truck with Mr. Witter. Orville slid his pigeons onto the back of the truck, then he covered the cage with canvas.

Tom saw two other cages sitting under canvas and heard the low murmur of pigeons.

As Tom and Orville climbed in front, Mrs. Breen handed Orville a large sack and a thermos. "Nice seeing you again, Helen," Mr. Witter called, as they drove out of the yard.

Orville's mother raised her hand to wave. Neither Orville nor Mr. Witter talked as they drove along Huntley Road toward the main highway. Tom was beginning to think all country people were tongue-tied—except for smart guys like Gary and Shorty. Even Dave said as little as possible when they were together.

Tom squirmed on the seat and wished the truck had a radio. He decided to watch Mr. Witter drive. Maybe he could learn something more. But Mr. Witter's truck was an automatic, and there was no shifting of gears.

"How many pigeons have you got back there?" Tom asked finally.

Mr. Witter rolled down his window and spat. "Got ten this trip," he said. "My best racers from last year."

Orville blinked his green eyes. "Real champions," he said.

"Trained most of them myself," Mr. Witter said. "That for a fact, Orville?"

Orville nodded.

Mr. Witter spat again and rolled the window back up. "Had good breeders to start with though," he added. "Right, Orville?" His voice was low and knowing.

Orville shrugged and said nothing. His eyes slid across

the unchanging countryside with the look Tom had noticed before.

By ten o'clock they had traveled the two hundred miles and rolled into the town of Savannah. Mr. Witter drove the truck through town and pulled in at a large truck stop on the outskirts.

"Good a place as any," he said. And Orville seemed to agree.

At the back of the truck stop, Mr. Witter parked the truck in an open area of pavement and got out. "Storm headed this way," he said, glancing up at the sky.

Tom wished he had brought the binoculars along. The sky looked clear and blue to him, with just a few white clouds in the distance. He wondered whether they were going to release the birds right at this spot.

Orville climbed onto the back of the truck and uncovered his cage. Mr. Witter did the same. Then he opened a small jar and shook a handful of rice into a flat dish.

"What's that?" Tom asked.

Mr. Witter opened one cage and offered the dish to the pigeons inside. "Wet rice," he said. "Keeps the birds from getting thirsty on the way home." He let each bird eat only a few grains, then took the dish away.

Orville uncapped the thermos and poured some water into a dish. He let each of his pigeons drink a little.

Next, Orville pulled a blue notebook from his jacket and handed it to Tom. "Write the time down as I release each bird," he said.

Tom opened the notebook and found each of Orville's pigeons listed by name. Next to each name were several columns in which Orville had noted the pigeons' flight times from the year before.

"Might as well start," Orville said.

He reached into the cage and lifted Blue Boy out first. Tom checked the second hand on his watch. As Orville tossed Blue Boy into the air, Tom wrote the time in the notebook next to the pigeon's name. Then Orville released Silver Bow. It took only a short time to toss all the pigeons into the air. Mr. Witter released two of his at a time. Then he wrote down their starting time in a book he'd carried in his coat.

When Orville tossed Grey Cloud into the air, Tom stood watching. "Good luck, Grey Cloud!" he called after the bird. Then he checked the watch and noted Grey Cloud's time in Orville's notebook.

He watched as Grey Cloud flew higher and higher over the parking lot. His grey wings stretched wide and his legs were tucked neatly beneath his body.

"Good luck!" Tom called again.

Mr. Witter closed his cages and folded the tarps. "Better get back on the road," he said. "We can eat on the way."

In the truck Orville unwrapped some sandwiches and handed one to Tom and one to Mr. Witter. They all ate as the truck sped along the highway north.

"I'm mighty hopeful about two of my grizzles," Mr. Witter said. "Got a blue check that shows promise, too."

At first Tom thought these were the names of Mr. Witter's pigeons. But as he talked more about his birds, Tom realized the words described a pigeon's color and markings. He wondered which type of pigeon Grey Cloud was.

When they had finished eating, Mr. Witter bit off a chunk of tobacco. Suddenly Orville bent forward, holding his stomach with both hands.

Tom frowned until Orville sat up again. "You okay?" he asked.

Orville nodded. "Ate too fast," he said simply.

Mr. Witter hummed to himself as he chewed on his tobacco.

"How long will it take the pigeons to get home?" Tom asked.

Mr. Witter pushed the tobacco into one cheek. "First bird might get back before three."

Tom figured quickly in his head—that meant a pigeon could fly about forty miles an hour.

"All the birds should be back by five," Mr. Witter added.

Tom hoped that Grey Cloud would get back first—that he would not get lost or shot at along the way. He looked out the truck window, hoping to see one of the birds on the way. But the highway curved and turned through the countryside. Anxious to reach their food and water, the pigeons would fly in a straight path north toward home. Tom felt sleepy and leaned his head against the back of the seat.

When he woke up, the truck was turning off the highway onto Huntley Road. Tom rubbed his eyes and glanced at the watch on his arm. It was almost three. At any minute the first pigeon would be coming across the fields south of Orville's loft.

Mr. Witter dropped Orville and Tom off at the mailbox. "Good luck, you boys!" he called.

Tom stopped to wave, but Orville walked straight to the loft. Inside, he opened the trap at the top of the loft and filled the coffee can with seed. Tom pulled out the blue notebook. He could hardly wait for the pigeons to start coming home.

Outside, Orville stood holding the can of seed and watching the sky to the south. Tom squinted hard. He wished he had not forgotten the binoculars. He glanced at his watch and then at the sky. It was after three o'clock and there was no sign of the pigeons.

"Where are they?" he said anxiously.

Orville shaded his eyes—just as the sun went under a cloud. "Might be raining south of us. Slow them up some," he said.

Then Tom saw a speck beyond the pasture. But it was only a blackbird.

Suddenly Orville begain shaking the can and whistling. Tom squinted hard but could see nothing. Then he noticed a speck growing larger every minute. "Here comes one!" he shouted. He hoped it would be Grey Cloud coming in first, home again safe and unhurt.

"It's Snow Arrow!" Orville shouted. He shook the can as though his arm would fall off and whistled through his teeth. When Snow Arrow heard the sound, he increased his speed.

Inside the loft Orville coaxed Snow Arrow through the trap with the pan of seed. Tom checked the watch and recorded the time in a column next to Snow Arrow's name. When all the pigeons were home, they would figure out each bird's time.

Tom looked down the row of figures Orville kept from last year. The records showed that Snow Arrow was usually the fastest racer. But Sun Shadow and Grey Cloud had also done well. Tom hoped that Grey Cloud's mended leg would not slow him down this year. If it had healed correctly, maybe he could beat them all. Tom hurried back outside to watch the sky.

At three-thirty, Tom spotted two specks in the distance. "Grey Cloud!" he shouted when they got nearer. It *was* Grey Cloud flying ahead, with Blue Boy trailing. Tom jumped up and down whistling and calling. Blue Boy was released ahead of Grey Cloud, and Grey Cloud had overtaken him.

The two pigeons circled the loft, glided downward, and landed on the outside perch. Then Grey Cloud hopped through the trap. Tom wrote the time beside Grey Cloud's name. He wondered how Mr. Witter's pigeons were doing. Did he have a pigeon flying faster than Snow Arrow and Grey Cloud?

At four o'clock, the last pigeon circled the loft and glided onto the perch. It was Silver Bow. He looked bedraggled and weary, and his feathers were wet. "Got caught in the storm, most likely," Orville said.

Tom looked at the huge thunderclouds gathered over the distant woods. "Home just in time," he said. He held the pan of seed close to Silver Bow's chest and watched him eat. Then he wrote his time in the notebook.

It was raining hard when Tom and Orville finished in the loft. In the house Tom sank on a kitchen chair, waiting for his father to pick him up. Orville stood at the stove, stirring a pan of soup on the back burner.

"Going out in the morning?" Tom asked.

Orville tasted the soup and nodded. "First race is in two weeks."

Tom heard his father honk ouside. "See you tomorrow then," he said.

10

On Sunday morning the sky looked threatening. Heavy clouds lined the woods to the south of Tom's bedroom window. He yawned and crawled deeper under the blankets, scrunching his pillow in a hump. He wondered what to do. He couldn't call to see if Orville was going to take the pigeons out.

Finally he dressed and went downstairs to the kitchen. "Might as well go over," he said to himself. He grabbed a hooded rain jacket and his father's binoculars, and hurried outside. A brief splash of sunlight danced over the yard. Tom got on his bicycle and pedaled to the main road. The clouds seemed to be heading away.

Halfway to Orville's, Tom passed a farmer in a combine that spread across both lanes. As Tom wheeled around him, the farmer tipped his hat and smiled. Tom waved back. Some country people could be friendly if they wanted.

Orville was pouring water into the pig's trough when Tom got there. The black-and-white cat wound around his ankles, crying loudly. "Fool cat!" Orville said. He reached into his overall pocket and tossed it a biscuit.

Tom watched the huge cat leap on the biscuit, biting and gulping it down. "A cat that eats biscuits beats all."

Orville turned laughing. "Old Caesar eats anything."

Tom helped Orville feed the horses and watched him

milk the cows before putting them out to pasture. The warm milk steamed as Orville's long fingers shot it into the bucket between his knees. Once more the cat sat begging at his feet. Orville squirted a long stream of milk straight at the cat's whiskers.

"There you go, Caesar."

The creamy milk dripped down the cat's chin, but he caught every drop. Then he sat washing his face with one paw. As Orville continued milking the cows, the cat followed him. It seemed to Tom that Orville knew how to do everything. He could swing a pitchfork. He could milk a cow or fix a pump. He could drive a truck.

By the time Orville finished milking, the weather had changed again. A row of rain clouds moved across the sky.

"Think the rain will miss us?" Tom asked.

Orville glanced at the sky. "Don't look too bad yet."

In the loft Tom placed Grey Cloud and a pigeon called Light Feather in the wire cage. When White Rain had been killed, Orville chose the white-winged hen to replace her in the races. Her head, neck, tail, and body were a dark solid grey. Only her wings were white, with a single streak of lighter grey.

Orville put Snow Arrow and the others in the cage and carried it into the yard. When he backed the truck out of the garage, the sun was shining again.

At the mailbox Orville paused a minute before turning onto the road. He leaned forward, pressing his stomach with one hand.

"Something wrong?" Tom asked.

Orville shook his head and shifted the truck into first gear. The truck rattled onto the road.

"Are we going to the quarry again?" Tom asked. He

held the blue notebook and the binoculars on his lap.

Orville nodded, and Tom watched him shift gears as they rounded a sharp turn. He was sure he could drive if he only had the chance. Sometimes after supper he sat in Dad's truck working the pedals. Dad said he could drive around the place as soon as he was old enough for a learner's permit. But that was years away.

Again he wondered how Orville got away with driving around the back roads. They passed a car with a camper hooked on the back, and Tom turned to Orville. "When did you learn to drive this thing?"

Orville stared at the road and pushed his glasses up on his nose. "Can't remember," he said at last.

Tom bet Orville remembered learning to drive, all right. He just didn't want to talk about things, as usual.

At the quarry road Orville slowed down and eased the truck over the narrow ruts. Last night's rain had made them muddy and more hidden than ever. Tom hoped they would not get stuck in the mud thirty miles from home. But Orville steered the truck over the ruts, and they pulled to a stop. Tom jumped out and hurried to the back. For a moment Orville sat quietly in the front. Tom saw him lean forward and rest his head against the steering wheel.

"Are you sick?" Tom called from the back.

Orville straightened up and stepped out of the truck. "Stomachache," he said. "Too many biscuits." He walked to the back and climbed up with Tom.

Tom thought Orville's face looked pinched and pale, but he said nothing. Instead, he opened the wire cage and reached in for one of the pigeons.

Sun Shadow was the first pigeon he tossed into the morning air. The pigeon's wings looked bluish-black as the sun splashed across them. Sun Shadow flapped his strong wings and rose above the quarry.

Tom reached for Grey Cloud in the back of the cage. "Hey, lazybones," he said.

Orville had already released Snow Arrow and Blue Boy. Grey Cloud rubbed his beak against Tom's hand as Tom lifted him in his hands. Once in the air, Grey Cloud rose easily on his wide grey wings. Tom watched through the binoculars as the pigeon turned to the east and disappeared. Then he put the notebook in his pocket and climbed into the truck.

Orville got in beside him and started the engine. Tom liked the feel of the old truck shifting gears. He liked the smell of the worn-out seats, and the way the front fenders curved. At the main road Orville stopped, then pulled onto the highway. They had gone only a few miles when Orville leaned forward suddenly. He clutched at his side, drove to the shoulder of the road, and stopped.

"Orville! What's wrong?" Tom grabbed Orville's arm and the steering wheel at the same time.

"My side hurts. It hurts real bad," Orville groaned.

Tom felt frightened and helpless. Orville's face was almost white, and his mouth was twisted with pain.

"I can't move!" Orville cried. "Help me!"

Tom jumped out of the truck and ran to Orville's door. He opened the door and swung himself up. "You've got to move over," he said, pushing at Orville's legs and shoulders.

Bending forward and holding his stomach with both hands, Orville slowly dragged himself across the seat. "It hurts," he cried again.

Tom slid behind the wheel of the truck. Without thinking he pushed in the clutch with his left foot, shifted into first gear, and eased his right foot onto the gas. The truck lurched forward, and Tom gripped the steering wheel. Orville groaned with pain as the truck lurched and lurched again. Somehow Tom got the old truck back on the road and into high gear. Before he knew it, he was turning into Orville's yard. Orville lay sideways against the passenger door, his eyes shut.

Tom leaned on the horn and jumped out of the truck.

"Mrs. Breen! Mrs. Breen!" he shouted, as he ran toward the house.

Orville's mother ran out of the barn, carrying a basket of eggs.

"Hurry up!" Tom yelled. "Orville's in the truck—and he's hurting bad!"

Mrs. Breen left her basket near the porch and ran to the truck. Between them they eased Orville from the truck and onto the ground.

"Ma," Orville groaned once, and closed his eyes.

"Get help!" Mrs. Breen cried to Tom. "Mr. Mason. Next farm over!"

Tom climbed back in the truck and drove out of the yard. At the mailbox he glanced back at Mrs. Breen cradling Orville's head in her lap. He remembered the Mason farm. He leaned on the horn as he rattled down the drive. A man and a woman hurried out of the house to see what was going on.

"Call an ambulance!" Tom shouted, as he pulled the truck to a stop. "Something's wrong with Orville Breen!" The woman dashed back into the house, and the man hurried toward the truck. "Let's get on back," he said as he climbed in.

When they reached Orville, Mr. Mason jumped out of the truck and knelt beside him. Orville lay quiet and ghostly with his head on a pillow while Mrs. Breen held his hand. Mr. Mason felt Orville's pulse.

"You were wise not to move him," he said.

Tom paced back and forth between the truck and Orville until he heard the ambulance siren in the distance. Then he hurried to Orville and knelt beside him. "I'll take care of the birds," he said. "Don't worry about it."

Orville nodded without opening his eyes.

Soon the ambulance arrived, and Orville was lifted onto a cot and inside. Mrs. Breen climbed in after him.

"Don't worry," Mr. Mason said. "We'll take care of everything here."

Tom watched the ambulance turn onto the road and speed out of sight in a cloud of dust.

Mr. Mason placed an arm across Tom's shoulder. "Quick thinking on your part, young man," he said. "Now if you'll drive me home, I'll come back later on and see to the chores."

Tom nodded. He put the pillow on the back porch and climbed in the truck. As they left the farmyard it dawned on him. He was driving! He was driving the truck by himself! He shifted gears and the truck jerked forward. Mr. Mason reached for the armrest and hung on.

"I don't drive much," Tom explained.

Mr. Mason patted Tom's arm. "You're doing fine."

On the way back to Orville's, Tom sat tall behind the wheel. He had driven the truck all the way back from the quarry with Orville sick beside him. He felt good knowing he had done the right thing in an emergency. He felt especially good about being able to handle the truck so well the first time. He fingered the gearshift knob with his right hand. In a way he hadn't lied to Gary Stevens at all. He really did know how to drive.

11

In all the excitement Tom had forgotten the pigeons. When he turned the truck into Orville's yard again, he saw them. Three or four were sitting on the roof of the loft. Several others sat on the perch outside the trap. No one had opened the trap for them when Orville got sick.

Tom parked the truck in the yard and hurried to the loft. As soon as he opened the trap, Grey Cloud and Sun Shadow popped through and headed right to their feed. The rest of the pigeons entered the loft close behind, and Tom wondered which one had gotten back to the loft first, as he filled the cups and poured fresh water into the watering trays.

Was it Light Feather? She cocked her small head sideways when Tom gave her fresh seed. Was it Blue Boy? He had no way of knowing, and the notebook would stay blank for today. Secretly he hoped Grey Cloud had flown faster than the rest—even faster than Snow Arrow.

Tom lowered the trap in place and latched it shut. He kept thinking about Orville lying pale and still on the ground. One of the ambulance attendants had placed an oxygen mask over Orville's face before they drove off. And Mr. Mason said it sounded like an appendicitis attack. Orville's mother was silent and wide-eyed, saying nothing. Tom remembered when his father had collapsed with a heart attack last year. His mother couldn't be still until help came.

Outside, Tom closed the loft door. Then he parked the old truck in the garage and slid the keys under the floor mat where Orville always kept them. When he stepped out of the garage, the cat darted around the corner and began rubbing against Tom's legs and yowling.

Mrs. Breen's basket of eggs sat on the ground. Tom picked up the basket, and the cat followed him across the yard to the porch.

Inside the house, Tom looked around for something to feed the hungry animal. In a corner a sack of dry cat food sat against the wall next to an empty bowl. The cat pushed at the bowl with his head and cried.

"Okay. Okay," Tom said. He filled the dish and put away the eggs as the cat ate hungrily. Then Tom gave the cat fresh water and went back outside.

Tom was in the barn giving the horses hay when Mr. Mason drove in. Tom ran outside to meet him.

"How is Orville?" he asked.

"Mrs. Breen called from the hospital," Mr. Mason said. "Orville had a ruptured appendix. Got there just in time."

Did that mean Orville might have died? "Is he going to be okay?" Tom asked.

Mr. Mason nodded. "Orville's mother will stay near the hospital till Orville is better," he said. "How are things going here?"

Tom shrugged his shoulders. "I can feed the pigs and all that," he said. "But you'll have to do the milking."

Mr. Mason laughed. "Just so you take care of those

blasted birds," he said. "Never liked them when Orville's father had them. Don't like them now."

"Orville's father raced pigeons?" Tom said.

Mr. Mason crossed the yard and stood looking out across the pasture where the cows grazed. "Had some real champions, so I understand," Mr. Mason said. He filled a pipe with tobacco, lit up, and began puffing.

Now Tom understood how Orville knew so much about pigeons. He had learned it all from his own father. Tom waited, hoping Mr. Mason would tell him more. But Mr. Mason stood puffing thoughtfully on his pipe.

"What happened anyway?" Tom asked at last. "I mean, to Orville's father." He felt his face flush and hoped he wasn't being too nosy.

Mr. Mason turned to Tom. "Reckon you're new around here. Don't know the local history."

Tom nodded. "We moved into the Reamer place last month." He waited for Mr. Mason to go on.

"Well, Henry Breen was in the war," he said. "Korea, guess it was. Got a piece of shrapnel in his head they couldn't get out. Finally worked its way to his brain." He drew a deep breath on his pipe.

Tom stared at Mr. Mason. "His brain?"

Mr. Mason nodded. "Got him in the veterans' hospital back in the city. Poor man don't even know his wife and kid no more."

For a while Tom and Mr. Mason stood silently staring out across the pasture. Then Mr. Mason turned and walked to the barn. Tom glanced about the neglected farm. Mr. Breen's brain was damaged—just like Gary Stevens said it was. Orville had never told Tom about it. That was the way Orville was—silent and strange, different from any boy Tom had ever known. Tom knew if

Gary's father had been wounded in a war, the whole world would think he was a war hero. Maybe Orville did not want to think about his father lying hopeless month after month.

The next morning at Orville's, Tom fed the pigeons and cleaned up the loft before school. He unlocked the house and filled the cat's dish by the stove. He had to hurry to catch the school bus at the end of Huntley Road.

He felt good knowing that Orville was going to be all right. As he started down the aisle, Gary reached out and grabbed his sleeve. "Hear your buddy's in the hospital." Gary grinned. "Did he flip out like his old man?"

Tom pulled his arm away. News sure traveled fast. Dave and Shorty looked up at him from their seats. "Since you know Orville is in the hospital, then you know why," Tom said.

Shorty laughed, slapping his knee. "That's telling him."

Gary gave Shorty a dirty look. "Yeah, had his appendix out."

Tom saw an empty seat behind Dave and sat down. It felt good to put old Gary in his place for a change.

But Gary swung around in the seat to say, "As long as he's in there, maybe he should have his brain examined."

Shorty and Dave laughed. It seemed they liked to laugh at anything. Tom shrugged his shoulders. "Guess there's nothing wrong with Orville's brain," he said. "Like I said before, he can drive a stick-shift truck already." Tom narrowed his eyes at Gary. "Can you?"

Gary turned pink around the ears, and his eyes snapped. "Anyone can drive if they got the chance," he said. "Except maybe you."

Tom clenched his fists. He didn't want to start a fight

on the bus—kids got dismissed from school for doing that. Instead, he straightened his shoulders and glared back at Gary. "I can drive, all right," he said. "I drove Orville back to the farm when he got sick." Tom stood up, walked to the back of the bus, and sat looking out the dirty window. He *could* drive, and he was glad he had told them all. Now maybe Gary would quit treating him like a dope.

An announcement during school study hall reminded everyone that there would be no school the next day, due to a teachers' workshop. Tom had forgotten about this extra day off, and he found himself making plans to work with the pigeons the next day. Maybe he would take them to the quarry for a training flight. Orville would be surprised when Tom told him about taking the pigeons out alone.

After school Tom went straight to the Breens' farm to help Mr. Mason with the evening chores. He filled the water trough for the pigs, slopped meal and soured milk into their feeding troughs, and then headed toward the pigeon loft. The evening was cool and clear, and Tom opened the trap so the birds could get some exercise. "Good boy," he called to Grey Cloud, as the pigeon popped through. Outside, Blue Boy and Silver Bow sat sunning on the perch before stretching their wings to fly.

Tom watched them glide and circle above the farmyard. Had any of these pigeons belonged to Orville's father? Snow Arrow sat on the peak of the roof, looking like a white weather vane. Orville had a special feeling for the snow-white bird. Now Tom wondered if Snow Arrow had been one of Henry Breen's champions before the shrapnel lodged in his brain.

Snow Arrow stretched his wings wide as Tom watched. The pigeon's eyes blinked golden as he ruffled his feathers in the sun. Tom thought of his own father. He remembered him lying in the hospital with a mask over his face and tubes running to a needle in his arm. What if Dad had never come home again? Where would he, Mom, and Carrie be by now?

The sun dipped behind a cloud to the south, washing the farmyard in a rosy light. Tom went inside the loft to fill the seed cups and watering trays. He put the cover on the feed can and waited for the pigeons to come in to feed. Snow Arrow popped through the trap first. Then came Blue Boy and Light Feather and the others. Grey Cloud came in last. Tom closed the trap, hooked it shut, and stood watching the pigeons eat. Then he closed the loft behind him and walked to the barn to help Mr. Mason carry the pails of milk to his truck.

12

The next morning Tom gulped a glass of milk before starting out from home. Except for a few thin clouds, the sky was clear again—a perfect day to take the pigeons out. In the afternoon he had to help Dad finish the new horse stalls in the barn. But now the morning was his. His legs were strong, and the bicycle sped along the familiar country roads. He could hardly wait to get to the loft and load the pigeons into the wire cage. His feet itched to work the clutch and gas pedals on the old truck again.

When Tom coasted into the yard at Orville's, Mr. Mason was coming out of the barn with two milk pails. He had let old Caesar out of the house already, and the cat wound around his legs. A little milk slopped over, and the cat lapped it from the ground.

Mr. Mason poured the rest into a large milk can on his truck. Then he locked Caesar back in the house and climbed behind the wheel. "See you later, Tom," he called, as he started out of the yard.

Tom waved. When the truck was out of sight, he jumped high in the air. He was glad he would have the place to himself. He didn't want Mr. Mason watching and laughing when he backed the old truck out of the garage.

In the loft the pigeons greeted Tom eagerly. They seemed happy to see him again.

"Coo, boys. Coo, girls," he said softly.

For the first time Snow Arrow landed on his outstretched arm. Grey Cloud landed on his shoulder, bobbing his head and cooing. The pigeons seemed to trust him now, and Tom felt in control. Gently Tom cupped Snow Arrow in his hands and placed him in the cage. "Time to get going," he said, making his voice slow and even like Orville's. When he had Grey Cloud, Silver Bow, and the others inside, he reached for the blue notebook. This was going to be a good morning. Orville would feel better when he knew that the pigeons weren't sitting around the loft all day.

In the garage he slid the cage onto the back of the truck and fished the keys out from under the mat. He opened the sagging door and climbed into the driver's seat. For a moment he sat feeling the curve of the steering wheel beneath his hands. Then he put the key in the ignition. The truck was already in neutral gear. He turned the key and pressed his right foot on the gas. Tom's heart raced at the sound of the old engine. He breathed deeply, pushed the clutch in with his left foot, and eased the gearshift into reverse gear. Soon he was moving out of the old garage as smoothly as Orville ever had. He pulled around, shifted into first gear, and headed out of the farmyard with the cage of pigeons.

On Huntley Road, Tom kept his eyes straight ahead. He stopped at the intersection south of the farm and rattled on down the road in the direction of the old quarry. He whistled as he drove along. The sun slid in and out of the thin clouds. "I'm driving. I'm driving!" he shouted out the open window.

When he reached the turnoff road for the quarry, Tom eased onto the brakes. He was glad the road was dry for a change. The truck bumped along, the ruts bouncing the cage on the back and rattling the old fenders. Tom stopped beside the quarry and climbed out.

On the back of the truck he opened the blue notebook and placed it on top of the cage. The first pigeon he lifted out was Silver Bow. Tom held the grey-streaked bird carefully and tossed him into the air. Quickly Tom checked his watch and wrote the time next to Silver Bow's name. He released Blue Boy and Snow Arrow next, and then Light Feather, jotting their starting times in the book. Last of all he lifted Grey Cloud out of the cage. "Good boy," he said softly. He brushed his face next to the pigeon's dark head and tossed Grey Cloud high into the air. For a moment Tom stood on the back of the truck watching the pigeon lift and glide. At times Grey Cloud seemed almost to vanish below the thin grey clouds. Tom grabbed the notebook and hurried back to the driver's seat.

Soon he was rattling and bumping along Huntley Road again. At the last curve Tom held the steering wheel tight and took the turn as fast as he could. The truck hugged the road without swerving, and Tom laughed out loud. He sailed into the yard, parked in the yard next to the loft, and swung out of the truck. He walked straight to the loft and opened the trap. Then he headed back to the house. There would just be time to feed the cat before the pigeons got back. He had just opened the kitchen door when he heard a racket from the road. Gary, Shorty, and Dave were wheeling into the yard on their bikes.

"Thought we'd find you here!" Gary shouted. Shorty

stood his bike up on one wheel and headed straight for the porch.

"Thought we'd come over for a driving demonstration," Gary laughed. He cut Shorty's bike off and sent him bouncing into a bush at the side of the house.

Tom stood on the porch, watching them uneasily. He should have known Gary and the others would make something of his bragging.

Gary leaned his bike against a tree and sauntered across the yard. "Well, there it is. That famous stick shift you brag about!"

Shorty scrambled out of the bush, grinning widely. Dave sat on his bike at the side of the house, scuffing his feet in the dirt.

Tom wished they would all leave. He wished he had parked the truck in the garage and locked it.

Gary swaggered to the truck, calling back to Dave and Shorty over his shoulder: "Come on, let's have a look."

Tom stepped off the porch. "You leave the truck alone!" he hollered at Gary.

But Gary had already opened one door and stood staring inside the old truck.

"It's an antique!" Shorty said.

"Antique! It's a piece of junk," Gary said. "I'll bet it doesn't even run." He kicked at the tires.

"You guys get out of here," Tom said. "This is private property." He wished now that Mr. Mason would come back.

"Hey, fellas. Let's climb in." Gary opened the door on the driver's side. Shorty and Dave climbed on the back where the pigeons always rode. Gary leaned against a front fender, grinning at Tom. "Come on. Show us how you can drive this thing!"

Tom crossed the yard to the driver's side of the truck and stood with his hand on the open door. "You guys get out of here. You've got no right."

All at once Gary reached in the truck and dangled the keys from one hand. "If you don't, I will," he sneered, holding the keys out to Tom. He was about to get in the driver's seat.

Tom grabbed the keys and climbed behind the wheel.

Gary hurried to the passenger's side and swung into the truck. "I don't think you can drive at all," he said.

Tom gripped the steering wheel. "I can drive all right."

"Then prove it!" Gary leaned back against the seat with his arms folded across his chest.

Tom turned the key, and the engine started. Then he pushed in the clutch, shifted into first gear, and eased onto the gas pedal.

"Here we go!" Shorty yelled from the back.

"I'll drive around the yard. That's all," Tom said. He circled the yard in first gear.

"Anyone can drive in a circle," Gary said, stamping on the gas pedal. "Let's see you take it on the road."

The truck careened across the yard. In the back, Shorty and Dave hollered. Tom clung tight to the wheel, steering the truck toward the road. Gary stamped on the gas again.

"Cut it out, Gary!" Tom yelled. "I'll drive."

Soon they were at the mailbox, with half the truck sticking out on the road.

"This is more like it," Gary said, as they started down the road.

In the back Shorty and Dave stood holding onto the

side of the truck. Tom drove to the first farm and turned around. "I've got to get back now," he said. The pigeons would soon be home.

"No way," Gary said. "We've got all day." All at once Gary swung his left leg across the floorboards and stomped on the brake. The truck wheels spun into the gravel, kicking stones up on the fenders. Tom's head jerked forward. "What are you doing?" he yelled.

In the back Shorty and Dave stomped their feet and hollered. "Let's see you back this thing up!" Gary demanded.

"You're crazy! You know that?" Tom yelled.

But Gary leaned across, his leg still pressing the brake pedal. "Anyone can drive forward. Let's see you back this crate up!"

Tom's hands felt like ice on the steering wheel. He glanced at the sky. The pigeons would be back to the loft by now. Most likely Snow Arrow was already inside waiting for his seed.

"Let's go!" Gary sneered.

Tom's knee trembled as he pushed in the clutch. "Get your leg out of the way!" he yelled at Gary. Tom moved the gearshift up, across, and downward. Then he pressed on the gas. The truck leaped forward. It was the wrong gear.

Gary muttered something as the sun visor swung into his forehead. In the back Dave and Shorty groaned. "I don't like this!" Dave complained loudly.

Tom moved the gearshift again. This time the truck shot backward toward a wide ditch along the side of the road.

"Let me out of here!" Shorty yelled. Shorty and Dave

fell sprawling into the bed of the truck.

Quickly Tom slammed on the brake and shifted back into first gear. Gary grabbed at the wheel and tried to put his foot on the gas pedal again.

"Stop it, Gary Stevens! Stop it or I'll slam you all right into a tree!" Tom warned.

The truck careened down the road in a zigzag pattern. Suddenly a car headed toward them around a curve.

"Look out!" Dave yelled.

Tom yanked on the wheel and slammed on the brakes. The truck was heading straight for the ditch. It stopped with two wheels hanging over the edge.

"Now see what you've done!" Tom cried.

But Gary was already out of the truck. Shorty and Dave hopped down from the back. "We're getting out of here!" Gary hollered.

Tom watched them run down the road toward the farm. He tried to back the truck out of the ditch, but the tires only spun in the loose gravel. His right knee trembled, and sweat glued his shirt to his back as he gripped the steering wheel. He would have to get someone to push while he steered. Good old Gary and the others had run out on him. He tried once more to spin out of the gravel, and the tires finally grabbed the road. He backed onto the road, put the truck in first gear, and started toward the farm. As he reached the Breens' mailbox, Gary, Shorty, and Dave sped past him on their bikes.

"Some driver!" Shorty yelled as he passed.

"We'll be back for another driving lesson!" Gary shouted.

13

Tom parked the truck in the yard and ran to the pigeon loft. When he opened the door Caesar came sauntering out. A grey feather clung to his whiskers, and blood stained the white fur around his mouth.

"No!" Tom cried. When Gary and the others rode into the yard, he had forgotten to feed Caesar and close him in the house. Now he raced to the loft and flung the door open. Loose pigeon feathers were everywhere. The feed can was knocked over. And, in some of the cubicles, the pigeons blinked their round eyes and quivered with fear.

Tom looked up. On a beam near the open trap sat Silver Bow, with Sun Shadow huddled close behind him. Blue Boy peered out of his perch near the top of the loft. As Tom looked around, he saw the body of one pigeon on the floor in the corner.

"No!" he cried again.

The pigeon's head lay twisted and bleeding. Its pure-white wings were bent and broken. It was Snow Arrow, and he was dead.

Fear clutched Tom's chest as he turned away from the sight. "Grey Cloud!" he shouted. He saw Light Feather and all the others now. But Grey Cloud's perch was empty. A few grey feathers fluttered across the floor of the loft. Near the door Tom saw a light trail of blood. He pushed the door shut and stared down at the floor. There, lying just behind the door, was the body of Grey Cloud. The grey wings were spread and the golden eyes were closed.

Tom sank to his knees. Tears flooded his face as he picked up the wounded bird. Blood stained the chest and one wing a dark red. "Grey Cloud," he sobbed. Just then the cat crept around the open door and meowed.

"Get out! Get out, you rotten cat!" Tom yelled. He kicked at the cat and stood up with the pigeon in his hands. A faint movement pulsed against Tom's palm as he stood holding Grey Cloud. Grey Cloud's heart was still beating. Quickly Tom lay the pigeon on a box while he closed the trap and hooked it securely. Then, carrying Grey Cloud close to his heart, he left the loft, closing the door behind him.

"Please don't die," Tom pleaded. He ran to the truck and lay Grey Cloud on the seat beside him. Then he started the truck and headed onto Huntley Road toward the Masons' farm. "Please, God," he sobbed, as he turned down the Masons' long drive. Tears rolled down his nose, and he wiped them off with the back of his sleeve.

He stopped near the house and gently lifted Grey Cloud in his hands. Then he ran to the door and yelled as loudly as he could. "Mr. Mason. Mr. Mason!" he cried.

Just then Mr. Mason stepped out of the barn beyond the house. "What is it, Tom?" he called.

Tom ran to the barn, holding Grey Cloud close. When he tried to explain, the words and sobs jumbled in his throat.

"Hold on there," Mr. Mason said, taking Grey Cloud in his hands. He hurried into the house and put the pigeon on a small table in the laundry room.

"Fill that pan with warm water," he said, rolling up his sleeves. "Hand me a clean rag."

Tom's hands shook as he followed Mr. Mason's orders. Mr. Mason dipped the rag into the water and rinsed some of the blood from Grey Cloud's wing. Then he cut the bloodied feathers away from around Grey Cloud's neck and chest.

"Is he dying?" Tom asked, as he watched. "Please don't let him die, Mr. Mason."

Mr. Mason's face was dark and sad. "He's in bad shape, Tom. But his wing's not broken, and he's breathing steadily. What happened, anyway?"

Tom wished his father were there. But even though Mr. Mason didn't like pigeons much, he seemed to know what he was doing with Grey Cloud. He got a bottle of antiseptic from the kitchen and poured it directly on the wounds.

"The cat got him," Tom said at last. He stepped close to the table and stared at the wound on Grey Cloud's chest. Then he let his fingers touch the still grey head. "That dumb cat got into the loft!" he said. "And I'll fix him. I'll fix him good."

Mr. Mason wrapped Grey Cloud in an old towel and handed him to Tom. "You take the truck back to Breens'. I'll follow and drive you on home."

Tom nodded. In the truck Grey Cloud was still. How hurt the grey pigeon looked, his heart pushing against his wounded chest. At the farm Tom parked the truck and carried Grey Cloud back to the loft. Inside, the rest of the pigeons huddled together, frightened and uncertain. Tom placed Grey Cloud on a shelf out of the way. "Coo, boys. Coo, girls," Tom said gently, as he righted the overturned feed bin. Next he began sweeping the spilled seed into a pile, trying not to look at the body of Snow Arrow nearby. Finally he knelt on the floor, feeling sickened and hopeless.

How would he ever tell Orville about Snow Arrow? How could he explain? Gently he lifted the dead pigeon and placed him inside the flight cage on the floor. Just then Mr. Mason's truck turned into the yard, and Mr. Mason honked. Tom hurried out of the loft with Grey Cloud, latching the door behind him. Tomorrow he would bury Snow Arrow near the woods with White Rain.

The cat streaked around the corner of the house when he saw Tom. "Just wait. I'll fix you!" Tom yelled after him. In Mr. Mason's truck Tom cradled Grey Cloud on his lap. Tomorrow he would fix Caesar for what he had done.

At home Dad looked at Grey Cloud and checked his wounds. "What happened?" he asked, shaking his head.

Tom shrugged. How could he tell Dad that he had left the loft unguarded to drive around with Gary and the others? "The cat got in. That's all," he said.

Dad frowned at Tom, then turned back to Grey Cloud. "Mr. Mason did all anyone could for the poor bird," he said.

"He's not going to die, is he, Dad?" Tom felt the tears starting again. Surely something more could be done.

But Tom's father shook his head. "He's hurt bad, Tom."

That night Tom carried Grey Cloud to his room and placed the bird in a box next to his bed. For a long time he stayed awake, not wanting to turn off the light or go to sleep. What if Grey Cloud died in the night with no one to help him? Tom looked down at the bruised body to make sure the pigeon was still breathing. He hated Gary Stevens for coming around when he wasn't wanted. And he hated the cat for what he had done to Snow Arrow and Grey Cloud. He swallowed hard as he watched Grey Cloud's small heart pumping against the matted feathers. At last Tom fell asleep.

The next morning he woke and jerked himself upright on the edge of the bed. In the box Grey Cloud lay on his side, his eyes still closed. Tom leaned over the box and touched the pigeon's wing. The small chest rose and fell steadily. Grey Cloud was still alive.

"It's all right. You're going to be all right," Tom whispered.

He didn't want to go to school at all; he wanted to stay home with Grey Cloud. But Mom insisted. She promised to take care of Grey Cloud herself. Dad drove Tom over to Orville's to take care of the other pigeons and help Mr. Mason with the chores. And Tom knew he had to bury Snow Arrow before school that morning.

At the loft Tom filled the feed cups and poured fresh water for the pigeons. But instead of eating, they peered out at him suspiciously. He coaxed each one, talking gently and holding out his hand. Silver Bow cocked his head sideways, and Sun Shadow and Light Feather paced back and forth on their perches. Finally Tom had to face the job of burying Snow Arrow. He picked up the flight cage and carried it to the door of the loft.

When he stepped outside, the cat crept out of the barn and yowled at Tom. Tom closed the loft door and set the cage with Snow Arrow's body on the ground. Then he watched as Caesar sauntered toward him. A terrible hatred for the cat filled him as it sniffed at his shoes and began rubbing its body against his ankles. He could still picture the grey feather and the blood clinging to the cat's whiskers. All at once Tom swung down and grabbed the huge cat by the neck. "I hate you!" he screamed.

The cat's eyes opened wide in alarm. Tom tightened his fingers about the cat's white throat. "I'll kill you!" he snarled. He squeezed his fingers deep into the cat's thick fur.

The cat twisted and flung its body about, frantically trying to free itself. But Tom held the cat firmly, watching it jerk and turn in his hands. All at once Caesar dug his front claws into Tom's forearm and gave out a blood-curdling cry. The green eyes bulged, and saliva strung from its mouth.

"My God!" Tom sobbed, suddenly letting go. For a second the cat lay heaving and panting; then Caesar righted himself and streaked across the yard to the safety of the barn. "What have I done?" Tom cried.

He knelt beside the cage, staring in at Snow Arrow's dead body. When he looked up, the cat was nowhere to be seen. It was not the cat's fault Snow Arrow was dead. A pigeon was his natural prey. The fault was Tom's. He had forgotten to shut the kitchen door when he drove off with Gary in the truck.

Tom buried Snow Arrow next to White Rain. For a moment he stood looking down at the ground. Would Grey Cloud soon be lying there, too, because of his own foolishness? He hurried back to the house, filled a bowl with food for the cat, and placed it on the back porch. Then he ran to catch the school bus at the end of Huntley Road.

14

"Well, well, if it ain't A. J. Foyt himself." Gary laughed as Tom started down the aisle of the bus.

Shorty reached out and tapped Tom's arm. "Yeah, Mr. Indy 500."

Tom felt the hatred well up inside him, and he brushed Shorty's arm away. It was really all their fault in the first place. If they hadn't come around without being wanted . . . If Gary hadn't forced him to take the truck . . . Tom walked straight to the back of the bus and sat down.

When he looked up, Gary and Shorty were turned in their seats staring at him. But Dave was coming down the bus toward him.

"Hey, Tom, they're only kidding," he said. "Can't you take a joke?" He pushed in beside Tom on the wide seat.

Tom shrugged and turned to the window without speaking. All he could think about was Grey Cloud lying half dead—and how he had almost killed the cat. His hands still trembled at the thought of it.

"Come on. Don't be a bad sport," Dave said.

Tom wanted to shove him away, push him right off the seat. A bad sport? Couldn't take a joke? "Why can't you leave me alone?" Tom glared at Dave.

Dave looked startled; then he jumped up and marched

back up the bus without looking back. For the rest of the ride Tom sat staring out the dirty window.

At lunchtime Tom called home from the pay phone in the cafeteria. But his mother could tell him only that Grey Cloud was still alive, nothing more.

After school he called again before catching the school bus. Grey Cloud was the same. At least he's alive, Tom thought. There was still hope.

At the farm he hurried to the loft. When he stepped inside, the pigeons were huddled on their perches. Only Silver Bow greeted him as usual.

"Coo, boys. Coo, girls," Tom said softly. He couldn't blame the birds for being cautious and frightened. Patiently he held out a handful of feed for Blue Boy and Sun Shadow. "It's all right now." He made his voice gentle and low. How terrible it must have been for the birds to watch the cat rip into Snow Arrow and Grey Cloud.

Finally Blue Boy stretched his neck forward and grabbed a piece of dried pea. Sun Shadow cocked his head and blinked his amber eyes.

Tom filled the other feed cups and poured cool, fresh water into the water trays. Then he opened the trap at the top of the loft. He had to get the pigeons back to normal—back to going through the trap without fear. For a while the pigeons sat watching Tom and eating. Not one of them started for the open trap, although the sun was warm and inviting.

Finally Tom closed the trap and hooked it securely. How was he going to tell Orville what had happened? And how were the pigeons going to race in two weeks if they wouldn't even leave the loft?

Outside, the cat peered around the corner of the

house. Tom crossed the yard and stepped inside to fill his dish near the sink. From the open door the cat watched Tom closely. He had not forgotten how Tom had choked him that morning.

"Come on, Caesar. It's not poisoned."

The cat waited until Tom stepped away. Then he dashed to his dish, turning to glare at Tom before eating.

Tom locked the house and started for home. The late April sun was golden pink in the western sky, covering the fields with a reddish glow. Along the new corn fields, redwing blackbirds called to one another. Tom did not notice the beauty about him as he pumped his bike toward home. His heart was sick and heavy.

In the kitchen Grey Cloud's box sat next to the warm radiator. Tom dropped to the floor and looked down at Grey Cloud. The pigeon's eyes were still closed and he lay as though dead. Tom's throat ached. "Is he—is he dead, Mom?"

"He's still breathing," she said.

Tom glanced hopefully at his father. "Dad, he's going to be all right?"

"If he would start to drink a little . . ." Dad's voice trailed off.

"I keep trying," Tom's mother said. She held out an eyedropper full of water. "Maybe you'll have better luck."

Tom placed the tip of the eyedropper next to Grey Cloud's beak. Slowly he squeezed a few drops onto the narrow opening. But the water trickled down Grey Cloud's matted neck and onto the cloth beneath him.

"Please, Grey Cloud. Drink something." Tom squeezed again, and the water ran off into the box.

Tom's father touched his shoulder and urged him away from the box. "You can try later. Now you should eat. Then I think it's time we drove into Princeton to see Orville."

Tom wanted to see Orville, all right. He wanted to tell him he hoped he would get better and be home soon. But he did not want to tell him about the accident in the loft. He didn't want to see Orville's face when he heard about Snow Arrow. "Maybe we should wait and go on the weekend," Tom said.

Dad shook his head. "The sooner you tell Orville everything, the better."

Tom stood staring down at Grey Cloud's still and wounded body. He wanted to tell Dad how it had happened—how he had driven the old truck and left the loft open, how Gary and the others had taunted him —but he could not. He wondered how he could ever face Orville.

At the hospital in Princeton, Dad parked the car and they rode up in the elevator to Orville's floor. Through an open door they saw Mrs. Breen. She was standing at the foot of Orville's bed. She looked different dressed in neat slacks and wearing her hair in curls. Orville was watching a TV set that hung on the wall opposite his bed.

"How're you doing, Orville?" Tom asked, as he stepped through the door.

Orville turned and blinked at Tom. His hair seemed yellow against the white sheets, and his face looked pale and thin. He pushed his glasses up on his nose. "Oh, hullo," he said.

Dad took Mrs. Breen's arm. "Why don't we let the boys talk? I'll buy you a cup of coffee in the lounge."

Tom watched Dad and Orville's mother walk down the hall toward the elevators. Then he crossed the room to Orville's bed.

"You look okay." Tom tried to smile.

Orville scratched his ear and shrugged. "Thanks to you." His green eyes blinked like fireflies behind his glasses.

For a moment Tom stood leaning against the bed. Then he stepped to the window and looked down at the street.

"How are the pigeons?" Orville asked. "Snow Arrow —guess he misses me some."

A commercial for a new mouthwash blared from the TV, and Tom watched the traffic below. His throat felt tight and sore, and his lips were dry.

Quickly he spun around from the window. "Orville, I've got to tell you. Snow Arrow. Grey Cloud . . . " He stammered as he faced Orville. His hands felt sweaty and cold at the same time.

Orville looked confused. "What about them?"

Tom swallowed hard. "Snow Arrow is dead." He could barely finish. "Grey Cloud is . . . hurt bad."

Orville pulled himself up against the headboard. He stared at Tom and fingered the collar of his hospital pajamas. "Dead?" he groaned. "Snow Arrow? Dead?"

Tom turned away. What could he say? How could he explain? "The cat got in the loft," he said. Then he stepped back to the window, not wanting to look at Orville's stricken face.

He heard Orville blow his nose and then he heard a muffled sob. But he didn't turn around.

"How did the cat get in?" Orville finally asked.

Tom's father had asked the same question. Now Tom turned to face Orville directly. "I was careless," he said.

Orville said nothing. Tom knew he was wondering why the loft was open—where Tom had been when the cat got in. But Tom could not explain. He didn't want Orville to think he was careless. But how could he tell him he had let Gary talk him into taking the truck? How would Orville feel knowing Tom cared more about driving than about the safety of the birds?

Orville turned his face away. "Snow Arrow," he sobbed from his pillow.

"The others are all right. Sun Shadow, Silver Bow." The room felt hot and small.

Orville grabbed a tissue from the bedside stand and blew his nose again.

Just then Mrs. Breen and Tom's father stepped back into the room. "Mrs. Breen tells me Orville will be home on Friday," Dad said.

Orville sat up and began flicking the remote control of the TV set. The programs flashed back and forth, and the garbled sound filled the room. Mrs. Breen stared at Orville and then at Tom. "Well, thank you for coming," she said.

Tom stepped to the door with his father. He looked back to see Orville lying with the pillow hiding his face, his glasses on his chest. Then he hurried out of the room without speaking and started down the hall.

"You told him about the pigeons," Tom's father said. Tom nodded.

At the elevator Dad pushed the down button. "He had to know, Tom—sooner or later."

Tom stared at the green elevator doors. Orville had to

know, all right, but he didn't know the whole truth. And Tom hoped he would never find out.

At home Tom leaned over Grey Cloud's box with the eyedropper again. He squeezed gently, and Grey Cloud's throat seemed to move. Tom tried again. This time Grey Cloud swallowed the water. "Dad! Grey Cloud is drinking!"

Tom's father watched as Grey Cloud swallowed the second time. "Looks like he's going to be all right."

That night Tom lay awake with Grey Cloud's box next to his bed again. Grey Cloud was going to make it. He tried not to think about Snow Arrow. He tried not to think about Orville lying alone in the hospital.

15

The next day Grey Cloud stood unsteadily in his box and tried to hop from one corner to the other. Tom's father had dressed the bruised wing and chest.

"As soon as the wing heals, he will have better balance," he explained.

Tom held the pigeon as he fed him bread soaked in warm milk and a few grains of seed.

Each day at the loft Tom fed and cared for the other birds, too. They seemed to grow more calm and acted almost normal. When he opened the trap, they began to hop through to the warm sunshine. The cat kept his distance, not wanting to take a chance with Tom again.

On the school bus Tom tried to ignore Gary and the others. One morning Gary stuck his leg out in the aisle as Tom started by. "How about another driving lesson?" he sneered.

"Yeah," Shorty added. "Maybe you can teach me how to back up."

Tom glared at Gary. Then he dug his heel hard against Gary's bare ankle, saying nothing.

For a moment Gary held his leg straight; then he pulled it back. "Think you're smart," he snarled.

Tom stared into Gary's angry face and walked by. At

the back of the bus he sank onto the seat. He hoped Gary and Shorty didn't come around when Orville got home.

On Friday Tom rode to Orville's before school to feed the pigeons. He stood in the loft holding Silver Bow on his forearm and offering Blue Boy feed from his other hand. Orville would be home by evening. And Tom wondered if he would be welcome at the loft at all. "Coo, boys. Coo, girls," he whispered. Sun Shadow flew across the loft to the screened area to sit in the morning sun. The other pigeons ate their feed and pecked at their wing feathers to clean them.

He would miss coming to the loft twice a day. And he would miss seeing the pigeons and being a part of things. But he would not blame Orville for wanting to keep him away.

After school Tom watched out of the bus window for Huntley Road. It would be some time before Orville was strong enough to train the pigeons on his own. And the first race of the year was only one week off. Orville would need him to help with things.

He got off the bus and walked slowly toward the farm. When he reached the farmyard he stood at the mailbox looking toward the loft. The farm looked as dilapidated as ever, and the loft needed painting, too. He crossed the yard and knocked on the kitchen door.

Mrs. Breen answered, dressed in her usual overalls and red sweater. She motioned him inside, happy to be in her cluttered kitchen again. From the clothes basket Caesar narrowed his eyes to slits and switched his tail. Tom knew it would be a long time before the cat forgave him.

"Orville's in the loft," Mrs. Breen said, smiling. "Doctor says he can start school Monday."

Tom nodded and walked across the yard to the loft. For a moment he stood in the doorway looking around. It was almost like the very first time he had come here. Orville stood inside with Silver Bow on his shoulder. The grey-and-white bird rubbed his head against Orville's chin and cooed softly. Orville talked in gentle whispers. "Coo, boy." Tom felt awkward and unwanted again. And he knew Orville was thinking about Snow Arrow.

"Welcome home," Tom said with false cheerfulness.

Orville looked around, still holding Silver Bow close to his face. Tom swallowed hard, and Orville blinked from behind his glasses until Tom looked away.

"I buried Snow Arrow next to White Rain," he said. Immediately he wished he had not spoken.

Orville's face grew dark and strange. Then he turned and opened the trap at the top of the loft.

"I've been letting them out some every day," Tom said. He scuffed his feet in the dirt, then stepped inside.

Orville nodded briefly. He filled the feed cups from the large can in the corner and poured fresh water into the watering trays. "Grey Cloud?" Orville set the water bucket down. "How is he?"

"He's better. His wing is healing. Some feathers are starting to grow back on his chest."

Tom stood watching as Orville walked about the loft. Then he heard Mr. Mason in the yard and hurried outside. "You just take it easy," he called back to Orville. "Mr. Mason and I will take care of the chores."

Tom followed Mr. Mason to the barn and opened a fresh bale of hay for the livestock. He grabbed the pitchfork from the wall and swung the hay neatly into the stalls. Next he lay clean straw for the cows and hurried to mix the mash for the hogs in the outside pen. When he had finished, he leaned against the fence watching the pigs eat. When he looked up, Orville was crossing the yard from the loft.

"Some farmer, all right," Orville said.

"He's shaped up right well." Mr. Mason stepped out of the barn, laughing. "For a city boy, that is." He carried a pail of milk into the house.

Orville leaned against the fence near Tom. Just then Tom saw three figures coming down the road toward the farm.

"Got to finish feeding the horses," he said quickly. He turned and started toward the barn, but it was too late. Gary had seen him.

"Hey, Tom. Don't run off now!" he shouted from the road.

Tom stood in the middle of the yard, wishing he were invisible. The three boys coasted into the yard kicking up a dust cloud behind them.

"Come to get our second driving lesson!" Shorty laughed.

Orville stood watching, his hands jammed into his overall pockets. Tom glanced around to see if Mr. Mason was nearby, but he had returned to the barn. Suddenly Gary spun his bike onto one wheel and steered it over a hump on the ground. The bike swung sideways, and Gary jumped off, letting it crash to the ground. Who did he think he was anyway? Evel Knievel?

Shorty and Dave leaned their bikes against the porch as Gary swaggered across the yard. "See they got you patched up again," he said to Orville. He turned to Tom.

"Been practicing reverse gear, or do you still drive around in circles?"

Tom glanced at Orville, but his face was closed and serious. Tom wished Mr. Mason or Orville's mother would come outside. Instead, Gary walked toward the garage and opened the doors. "How about another buggy ride?"

Tom ran to the garage. "You can't go in there. This is private property." He wished Orville would say something.

Gary shoved Tom away. "We got your permission to look at your old truck, ain't we, Orville?"

For a moment Orville stood watching. Then he pulled his hands out of his pockets and walked to the garage. "Just what is it you fellas want?" he asked.

"We want old Tom here to take us for another ride," Gary said.

"Yeah," Shorty said, "without dumping us in the ditch again."

Orville turned to Tom. His green eyes looked like deep pools as he stood waiting for Tom to speak.

"They came over when you were in the hospital," Tom said finally. "They wanted a ride in the truck."

Gary shrugged. "Tom told us he could drive. He took us all for a little ride while you were away."

"Sure," Shorty said. "He bragged about how he could handle this old truck."

Orville stood looking from one to the other.

Tom clenched his hands into fists. "That's not true. I never offered them a ride. They *made* me take the truck out on the road."

Gary's smirk almost split his face in half. "Didn't hold a gun to your head," he said.

"Oh, no!" Tom yelled at him. "You grabbed the keys, said you would drive the truck yourself unless I came along."

"Sure, sure," Gary said and continued to smile at Orville.

Tom looked from one boy to another. They all knew the truth.

"Don't look at me." Shorty laughed. "I'm an innocent bystander."

Tom turned to Orville. "They kept saying you were a creep—crazy—stuff like that. I told them you were smart enough to drive."

A dark frown filled Orville's bony face. He pushed his glasses up on his nose and scratched his ear. "What folks say don't hurt me," he said.

For a moment they all stood looking at Orville. Gary hooked his fingers through his belt loops, and Shorty shook his head. Then Dave stepped forward. "Tom's right. We *did* talk him into taking the truck."

Gary shot Dave a nasty look. And Orville crossed to the garage and shut the doors. "Be no driving lesson today," he said.

"Hey, come on, Orville." Gary reached out to grab Orville's arm. Shorty leaned against the garage door. Just then Mr. Mason stepped back out of the house.

"Ho, what's going on here? A convention?"

"We got to get going," Gary said. He started across the yard, with Shorty and Dave right behind him. Gary and Shorty jumped on their bikes and spun out of the yard.

For a moment Dave sat with his feet touching the ground. "Glad you're okay, Orville," he said finally. Then he wheeled out of the yard to catch up with the others.

Mr. Mason stood holding another pail of milk and staring after them. "What was that about?" he asked.

"Ain't nothing," Orville said. He jammed his hands back in his pockets and headed back to the loft. At the door he turned to Tom. "You coming?"

Tom raced across the yard and into the loft behind Orville. He wanted to tell Orville the whole story. He wanted to get it all clear once and for all.

"Gary grabbed the keys, and the cat got out of the house," he began.

Orville took the blue notebook off the shelf.

"I left the trap open and—" Tom went on.

"Never mind all that," Orville said, glancing at the book. "We got work to do."

16

Orville and Tom worked with the pigeons all weekend. They drove to the old quarry and released the birds that Orville would enter in the first race of the year.

Tom said no more about Gary and the truck. And Orville was his quiet self again. Tom jotted the flight times of the pigeons in the blue notebook. But the pigeons were not flying as well as they had before the accident in the loft. Without Snow Arrow and Grey Cloud they seemed to lose heart. Tom wondered how they could possibly compete with Mr. Witter's birds.

Grey Cloud stayed in the box in Tom's kitchen; he still favored one wing as he hopped about. It would be weeks before he could fly again.

On Wednesday Orville carried a wooden box from the house and placed it in the loft. He raised the cover and lifted out a strange contraption. Tom noticed a clock on one end and several strange dials on the side. Directly on top was a small hole and some sort of a key. Orville dusted it with the sleeve of his shirt.

"What is that?" Tom asked. He tried to peer into the opening on the top.

Orville explained that the box was a timer for pigeon racing. Each pigeon owner had one. On the night before an official race, each pigeon had a race band stamped in his owner's timing clock. That way the race was fair and equal. Orville let his fingers rest on the timer as he talked.

Tom noticed a small brass plate at the front of the timer. HENRY BREEN was engraved on the plate. The clock had belonged to Orville's father. Tom wondered how long ago Mr. Breen had raced his own pigeons. Was Snow Arrow one of his original birds? Was that why Orville had loved that particular bird more than the others?

Orville placed the timer back in its box and polished the wooden case with a rag. Then he opened a cabinet and slid the timer inside.

On Friday Tom stepped off the school bus on Huntley Road and hurried to Orville's. It was the day before the race. Tom's father had promised to drive them to Mr. Witter's that evening to check in Orville's birds. When Tom reached the loft, he found that the birds had already been fed and were flying outside in the sunlight. Orville was nowhere in sight.

Tom crossed to the barn. Maybe Orville had started doing the chores without him. In the barn the horses stamped their feet as they chewed on the fresh hay in their stalls.

"Hey, Orville?" Tom called. He stepped outside again and looked about the farmyard. At the edge of the woods Orville was leaning against the sagging fence. He was looking down at the spot where Tom had buried Snow Arrow next to White Rain.

For a moment Tom stood still, not knowing what to do. He could guess what Orville was thinking—how Snow Arrow could have been flying in the race tomorrow. How his birds might have given Mr. Witter's a real race. If Snow Arrow had not been killed and Grey Cloud hurt so badly, Orville just might have had a chance. He crossed back to the loft and began scraping at the empty perches. Suddenly Silver Bow popped through the open trap and sat looking at Tom. The bird cocked his head to one side and blinked his amber eyes.

"How about you?" Tom said, holding out his arm.

Silver Bow hopped on and rubbed his head against Tom's wrist. "Think you and Blue Boy can fly as well as Mr. Witter's champions?" The grey-streaked pigeon bobbed his head up and down as if nodding yes. Tom scooped up a handful of seed for the bird. Wouldn't it be something if Silver Bow did win?

That evening Tom's father drove him back to Orville's. He waited in the truck while Tom and Orville loaded the pigeons into the wire cage. The birds would get nothing to eat until they returned from southern Illinois the next day. Orville fed them a mixture of corn and dried peas and a little rice soaked in water. The next morning they would each get a small drink of water before the race.

Gently Tom cupped Sun Shadow in his hands before placing him in the wire cage. "Good boy. Good bird," he whispered. He hoped with all his heart that one of Orville's pigeons would come home a winner. But more than that, he hoped they would all come back safely. He placed Sun Shadow in the cage with Silver Bow. Orville held Light Feather and carried her to the cage. The last pigeon to go into the cage was Blue Boy, and he cooed softly as Orville lifted him from his perch.

Finally they were ready. Tom carried the cage out, slid it onto his father's truck, and covered it with the canvas. Orville brought along the timing clock and the blue notebook. Soon they were all headed down the main highway toward Mr. Witter's farm.

Most of the county pigeon meetings were held at Mr. Witter's. As the biggest breeder and racer in the area, he would haul everyone's pigeons south to Savannah that night. The next morning the birds would be officially released by a pigeon-club official there.

About a dozen men were gathered in Mr. Witter's big barn. One man checked each timing clock for accuracy. Another filled out printed forms at a large table. Orville carried his timer across the barn while Tom watched everything that was going on. An excitement filled the air. Men and boys talked all at once as they filled out their race forms and waited for their clocks to be locked and sealed.

It seemed confused and complicated at first. Then Tom saw that each member had a set of rubber leg bands for his birds. The bands were stamped in the clock at the top opening. Then a band was stretched over each bird's left leg. When the bird returned to his home loft the next day, the band would be removed by the owner. Then the owner would place the band in his clock and a mechanism inside would stamp it with the exact time.

"How do you know who the winners are?" Tom asked.

Mr. Witter showed him one of the race sheets. "Each owner has his flight line officially measured," he said. He went on to explain that a flight line was the direct route across country from the release spot to the owner's loft. At the end of the race, the pigeon's flight time would be divided into the distance traveled. The pigeon that covered the most yards per minute would be the winner.

Other pigeons would win second, third, and fourth places.

At last Orville's pigeons were clocked and banded like the rest. Orville filled out the necessary forms. Then Tom saw Orville hand one man several bills from his pocket. Each member had to pay to race his birds with the club. That was how the club collected prize money for the winning owners. Tom wondered how much money Orville had to spend in order to have a chance to win.

Orville carried his cage of pigeons outside into the lighted yard. Pigeons were in cages everywhere. And more owners were still arriving.

"How many pigeons fly in this race? A hundred?" Tom asked. He followed Orville across the yard.

"More like two or three hundred," Orville said.

Tom's father waited near the truck. "I've seen some owners come in with two and three cages," he said.

Orville nodded. "Mr. Witter races twenty birds himself."

Tom wondered how Orville expected his pigeons to win. Four little birds against hundreds. Orville set his cage next to the others waiting to be loaded into Mr. Witter's huge truck.

Tom knelt beside it. Blue Boy and the others sat with their heads tucked beneath their wings. But Silver Bow blinked his round eyes in the yard light.

"We're counting on you," Tom whispered so no one could hear. He placed his fingers between the cage wires and touched the pigeon's wing.

Tom's father started the truck, and Orville climbed in. "You coming?" he called to Tom.

"Lead them all home," Tom whispered. He stood up and hurried to the truck.

On the way back to Orville's, Tom thought about Grey Cloud with his bruised wing and chest. And Snow Arrow lying dead at the edge of the woods. When he glanced at Orville on the seat beside him, he felt strangely sad. Orville wanted to win. He needed money to feed and care for his pigeons. But most of all, Tom thought, Orville needed to know that his father's birds were still champions. Tom glanced at his own father behind the wheel of the truck. In the darkness he couldn't see his father's face. But he knew it was content and healthy-looking. For the first time Tom admitted to himself he was glad they had moved to the country.

At the farm Orville stepped out and started toward the house.

"What time should I come over?" Tom called. He knew the birds would be released early from Savannah.

"Soon's you like," Orville answered. He made a tall shadow crossing the yard alone. Tom slid across the seat of the truck to watch his father drive the rest of the way home.

17

Race day dawned clear and cool, with only a few feathery clouds in the sky. Tom carried Grey Cloud's box to the kitchen. The pigeon stretched his good wing wide and bobbed his head up and down. It was time to take him out of the box so he could exercise more; time to take him back to Orville's loft, where he belonged.

At the stove Tom's mother turned pancakes on a griddle and lifted crisp bacon onto a plate. "You'd better eat plenty," she said. "You'll be too busy the rest of the day."

Tom sat down with Dad and Carrie. "I'm taking Grey Cloud back today," he said. "I'm taking him back to the loft with the others."

After breakfast Tom carried Grey Cloud outside in his box. He strapped the box to his bicycle basket with a strong rope. Then he pedaled out of the yard and down the familiar roads to Orville Breen's.

It was the first Saturday in May, and the sun was warm on Tom's shoulders. He unzipped his jacket and held his face into the warm breeze. All around him the earth seemed to reach for the sun. Along the roadside wildflowers bloomed in clumps against the fences. Trees were in full leaf now, and Tom filled his lungs with the smell of the country.

When he reached Orville's, he leaned his bike against the back porch. He untied the box and carried Grey Cloud to the loft.

Inside, Orville stood scraping the empty perches of the racing pigeons.

Tom stepped inside. "I brought Grey Cloud home," he said. He set the box on the floor and lifted Grey Cloud onto his old perch. The pigeon hopped around eagerly, poking his head into his empty feed cup and looking all about.

"What a sight." Orville laughed. He scooped a handful of seed from the large feed can.

Grey Cloud hopped to Orville's palm, eyed him cautiously, and then began eating. He seemed happy to be back where he belonged. He didn't seem afraid. Maybe he didn't remember anything about the accident with the cat.

It was too early for the racers to be coming back to the loft. The pigeons would have been released about eight that morning from Savannah. That meant several hours to wait before the two boys would start watching the sky to the south of the loft. The timer clock was ready on the shelf at the end of the loft. And Orville had the blue coffee can filled and waiting nearby. Tom slipped Dad's binoculars out of his jacket pocket.

"Waiting's the hard part," Orville said. He returned to scraping the perches and brushing the pigeon droppings out into a garbage bag on the floor.

Every few minutes Tom stepped outside to look at the sky. He shielded his eyes and held the binoculars to his face. He knew it was silly—watching ahead of time—but still, he wanted to look. He was watching the trees at the edge of the woods when the cat crossed the yard from the house. Tom saw him crouch low at the corner of the garage. At first Tom felt like chasing him away. But Caesar began creeping toward him, moving cautiously with his eyes narrowed and tail twitching.

"Come on, Caesar, I won't hurt you," Tom said.

Slowly the cat came toward him. At last he meowed loudly and wound himself between Tom's legs.

Tom reached down and patted the cat's huge head. "Guess we're friends again?" he asked.

Caesar rubbed his head against Tom's ankle, purring like a motorboat. Tom scratched the cat's ear and gently lifted him up. Then he carried Caesar back into the house where he would be safely out of the way.

It was nearly noon when Orville stepped into the yard and glanced across the sky. Tom lifted the binoculars. A chicken hawk glided over the cornfield, banked, and dove into the grass. And across the pasture a brown-and-black meadowlark sang from a fence post.

"There's one comin'!" Orville shouted suddenly. He pointed to the south and ran into the loft for the can full of feed.

Tom swept the binoculars across the sky, but he saw nothing. Then he focused on a spot just above the edge of the woods. He saw it! The first pigeon was flying straight toward them—a grey spot against the morning sunlight. Was it Silver Bow? Or was it Blue Boy? It was hard to tell if the grey feathers were light or dark in the distance.

Orville pulled the cap over his wiry hair and began shaking the can. "Come on. Come on." He whistled softly through his front teeth.

"Which one is it?" Tom asked, still watching through the glasses. He saw another bird just over the trees flying fast as the wind.

"It's Silver Bow," Orville said. He shook the can hard. "And Blue Boy right behind."

Tom watched the second pigeon gain speed as the two birds neared the loft. When they were directly overhead, Orville raced inside. Tom could hear him shaking the can and whistling. The pigeons circled briefly and glided downward. Tom hurried inside to help. As he stepped through the door Silver Bow popped through the trap, and Orville cupped him tight in his hands. Quickly Orville pulled the rubber race band off the pigeon's leg and slipped it into the opening at the top of the timer.

Next Blue Boy hopped through, and Tom held him fast. Orville released Silver Bow and removed the band from Blue Boy's leg. Both birds hurried to their perches, where fresh feed waited.

Back outside, Tom scanned the sky to the south again. Another pigeon appeared at the top of the trees, heading for the loft.

"Here comes one!" Tom yelled to Orville.

Then he saw the last pigeon a short way behind. "They're all home!" he shouted.

Orville dashed out of the loft, shaking the can and squinting. His strawlike hair poked out in all directions, and his long arms flung about like a windmill. Tom watched him set his mouth and whistle to the birds.

Sun Shadow glided onto the perch and popped through the trap. Tom and Orville worked together to pull off the racing band and clock it in the timer. Then Light Feather hopped into the loft. Orville held the white-and-grey

female while Tom removed her band.

Tom sighed when they were done. It had been exciting. Grey Cloud hopped back and forth, greeting each pigeon. The bird was glad to be back, Tom thought.

Orville placed the timer into the wooden case and closed the trap securely. "Excitin' part is just comin' up," he said. "Got to take the timer back to Witter's loft."

Tom waited in the yard while Orville backed the truck out of the old garage. Then he climbed in the front seat beside him. He wanted to ask Orville how he could drive without a license. But if Orville wanted him to know, he would tell him. When they reached Mr. Witter's, they saw several other members of the pigeon club carrying their timers into the barn. Orville parked the old truck, and Tom followed him inside.

About two dozen men stood around the barn, talking loudly and laughing together. The officials sat behind a long table. One official was opening a timer, as the owner waited. He lifted out a roll of paper and handed it to the man next to him.

Tom watched as the second man looked at the paper and wrote something on a sheet in front of him. Then he stepped to a blackboard nearby.

An air of excitement filled the large barn. Mr. Witter laughed loudly every few minutes and kept glancing at the board. Tom saw that on the board was a list of pigeons and their flight times.

"You're in the money this race, Witter," someone joked.

Mr. Witter laughed again. "Got the first three places won so far."

Tom saw Orville glance at Mr. Witter with envy.

"It's not over yet, Witter," another man called from across the barn. "It's not just time—it's distance."

Tom stood beside Orville as the official at the table opened his timer. Orville blinked rapidly when the man pulled the roll of paper out and handed it over. The second man adjusted his glasses and wrote quickly on the sheet. His face broke into a wide grin as he slid his chair back from the table.

"Better cancel that second-place money, Witter!" he hollered. He stepped to the board and wrote quickly. Then he turned to Orville. "You got yourself second place, son."

Orville rubbed his chin and scratched his ear.

"You've won!" Tom shouted. He grabbed Orville's arm and pumped it up and down.

Orville grinned, and the man at the table leaned forward and shook his hand. "Just as good as your old man," he said. "Something special about a Breen bird."

Several of the others crowded around, pounding Orville on the shoulders and cracking jokes. "Ain't won yet," Orville said.

The man at the table shook his head. "Only two more to check in. And they haven't been in the money yet."

"How much money did you win?" Tom asked.

Orville blinked his green eyes. "Enough," he said. He crossed the barn to where Mr. Witter stood talking with friends.

"I'd like to buy my pa's birds back now," Orville said. "That was the agreement."

Mr. Witter turned and spat tobacco on the dirt floor. "Right you are, son," he said, "that was the agreement."

Tom stood watching. Now he understood about

Orville's pigeons. They had belonged to his father before he went away for good, and Orville had been forced to sell some for feed money, until he could race pigeons himself.

Soon the men began leaving the barn. Orville and Mr. Witter stepped outside together, and Tom waited. When Orville came back into the barn he carried a box with four pigeons inside.

"My Pa's own breeders," he said. "Two pair."

Tom glanced at the pigeons in the box.

"Snow Arrow!" Tom said without thinking, for one bird looked exactly like the dead pigeon.

Orville held the box close. "Snow Arrow's brother," he said.

Orville collected his prize money and paid Mr. Witter. Then he walked out of the barn to the old truck. As they drove back to the loft Tom felt let down. The first race was over. Orville had bought his pigeons back again. Grey Cloud was almost healed and glad to be where he belonged. Tom knew he should feel happy, too.

At the farm Orville carried the four pigeons into the loft. He lifted them out of the box one by one and placed them on the perches he had cleaned that morning. The pure-white bird hopped onto Snow Arrow's old perch. The grey female sat on the perch next to Sun Shadow.

"Ought to have some fine young birds next spring," Orville said. He filled their feed cups and poured more water in the trays.

Tom felt a lonliness well up inside of him. "Guess I'd better get home," he said, "and help Dad with the new horses."

Orville stood back admiring his birds. "We can race

every week now, till fall," he said.

Tom watched Orville reach up to Grey Cloud's perch. Gently he cupped his hands around the grey pigeon and held him close. "Got a chance to win other races now."

Tom nodded. There *were* other races, and Grey Cloud would probably win some, too. He reached out and let his fingers touch the pigeon's light-grey head.

"You gonna take your bird home till he gets well?" Orville asked suddenly. He held Grey Cloud out to Tom.

"My bird?" Tom felt a lump rising in his throat as he took the pigeon in his hands. "Mine?"

"Seems like he's been yours since the day you found him in the field," Orville laughed. "Soon as he's strong, you can race him yourself."

Tom held Grey Cloud against his chest, stroking the bird's good wing gently.

"Might give the Breen birds some competition." He laughed.

Orville stepped to the white bird that looked like Snow Arrow. "We'll see about that, won't we, White Wind."

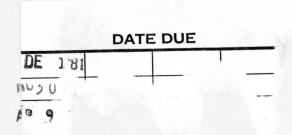

DATE DUE

DE 1 '81

NO 30

AP 9